THE
WORSLEY PLAGUE

LIZZY LLOYD

authorHOUSE®

AuthorHouse™ UK
1663 Liberty Drive
Bloomington, IN 47403 USA
www.authorhouse.co.uk
Phone: 0800.197.4150

Published by AuthorHouse   08/25/2017

ISBN: 978-1-5246-8034-3 (sc)
ISBN: 978-1-5246-8033-6 (e)

Print information available on the last page.

About the Author

LIZZY LLOYD GREW up in leafy Surrey in the 1960s. Surrounded by romantic woodlands and attracted to urban sophistication she had a magical childhood where reality and psychic experiences blended to create a rich imaginative spirit which was realised into stories, poems and songs. Her education spanned art school, couture fashion and photo editing before she took up a career in social justice for 35 years.

Her experiences of ancient places, buildings and an increasing insight into spiritual matters allowed her to develop novels which tantalise with their almost reachable possibilities.

Influenced by the great imaginers such as Nigel Kneale, Daphne DuMaurier and Shakespeare she found the books wrote themselves as if an invisible hand drove her own.

Her first novel, The Long Man, tells of Colin whose emotional breakdown draws him through the veil to the other side where he meets peoples from the ancient past, eventually sharing his days with Romans and Pagans. He discovers new life, love, talents and skills he did not know he had.

Her second novel, The Whyte Hinde, is altogether a deeper, darker exploration of the psyche. Where an intense passion with a handsome but cold man drives her to seek passion in the past where she is drawn back by a mysterious mansion that survives half in the present and half back in time. Her desires drive her to seek her lover in different times past, leading to a terrifying conclusion.

The Worsley Plague tells of two worlds, four hundred years apart, that collide when a mysterious disease overtakes the residents of a small country town, and whose origin lies in the history of the town and its previous occupants.

Read any of Lizzy Lloyd's books and be enchanted. Is the other world really so far from our door?

APPRECIATION

MANY THANKS TO Anthea Foden for the original idea; to Elaine McMahon for the technical and typing support and to Clare Eastland for her dedication and professionalism in the edit.

CONTENTS

CHAPTER ONE

LITTLE MEADOWS

"WE'VE GOT ANOTHER one, Gov". The telephone caller crackled into DI Mustoe's early morning coffee break, his iced bun hovering lusciously before his lips, the large mug of Nescafe steaming before him and now he was expected to discuss a case. It went through his mind to say "Not now Benson, I've got someone with me," and a struggle for a few seconds got the better of him but he relented.

"OK. Where's this one been found? He didn't need to ask. Two weeks before, in the small town of Worsley, a body was found covered in sores and ulcers where the injection sites had been infected. Although there had been no lock on the door, no one had reported it for a week although they felt quite sure numerous other users had been there during the week, taken a look and run off without telling anyone for fear of arrest for drug dealing. Consequently the flies had got in and feasted on the sores, maggots beginning to form in places. The weather had been hot for May anyway and a week had turned the flat into a seething mess of infection.

Specialist staff had had to be employed to clear the place after they moved the body; blood on the few items of furniture, an old sofa, a dirty mattress and sleeping bags. There was nothing left in the kitchen. Even the boiler had been ripped out, to sell, no doubt. The council had simply boarded it up and forgot about it. While flats in Gloucester were at a premium no one wanted to move out to the small Worsley council estate unless they were desperate or running away from something worse.

There survived a number of single parents whose behaviour or friends had been so persistently anti-social they had been evicted from city properties. Their last chance had been to accept a Worsley maisonette. Sure, the flats were quite large, but there were no shops, launderette or nightlife near the estate. It had been built near an old aerodrome a mile away from the town with just the concrete road and a bus stop with a bus twice a day to and from Gloucester. The town consisted of one mini market, a chemist, a general store geared to farmer's needs, a fish and chip shop and four pubs of diminishing respectability.

The occupants of Little Meadows were left much to their own devices. Children who were on the borderline of being "at risk" were left with their mothers because Social Workers did not know which to start with. Somehow the children survived, although Helen Bourne, recently out of training, knew they had seen worse sights and witnessed more violence than she had ever done. All she could do was visit as often as her large caseload allowed, which was once a week to visit the most needy families.

Helen was more than aware of the drug problem. Over the last two or three years it had leaked out of Gloucester like sewage spreading into the suburbs then to the nearer villages until every part of the countryside had its known dealers and victims. Little Meadows was the most affected. Its unpopular location only attracted those who had no choice in Local Authority housing. The addicted, the violent and the dispossessed. Initially they had tried to place people by category, elderly in one block, young Mums in another, single men in the tower block, in the faint hope that they might befriend each other and form support networks. Inevitably the single men had battened on the single mothers, sleeping in their beds, eating their food, using their electric, their own flats all but abandoned. In a few weeks when the first flush of lust had worn off the violence began and they swapped for the next willing female. Lonely girls looking for love cried for a bit then steeled themselves for the next bloke. The tower block became a target for people venting their hatred and frustration. Defiled and damaged it soon became uninhabitable even by the drunks.

The elderly who were in one-bedroomed bungalows did befriend each other but the noise, damage and violence after dark had sent them scuttling into their homes by 4pm; locked in and lonely, scared even to go next door for fear of being mugged. The police had given security advice but now they were trapped behind Chubb locks and bolts, door chains and emergency alarms for fifteen hours a day.

Then the drugs arrived. First the single men, with their friends and acquaintances who stayed overnight, then never went home. They introduced cannabis and amphetamines to the girls and in that euphoric state it was easy to get them on to heroin. The interminable boredom and isolation of Little Meadows was soon blotted out by the bliss of opiates, first smoked, then injected when the first impact started to wear thin. No need to go down the pub now, no one to complain and give you dirty looks, no one to question you where you'd dumped the kids. You could do it in the comfort of your own home, in front of the telly with your mates round you. If you had the money. Then when you needed more and more so there was not any money left for food you could hand over your child benefit book. If you had three kids that was £35 a week, enough for three bags a week. After that you could hand over your benefit book, ninety pounds a week, plenty for most, but managing on the child benefit for food was impossible but as long as the kids got a school meal they could manage on bread and marg at home.

If the bills mounted up and you were game for it the dealers gave you stuff, paid for in kind. All the girls hoped to get the not too bad looking guy, the one who seemed to control his drug use better, who was relatively clean and who did not give you a black eye in front of the kids, but that would be a good day and few on the estate were like that.

Most of the locals in Worsley, who had been born and raised there with either farm jobs or transport to go to Gloucester or even Bristow, lived in a suppressed outrage about the estate. No one visited except the reluctant trail of social workers, health visitors and probation officers and even they went in pairs. By the late 1980's there were no resources for Worsley, no beat officer or community bobby. Every night a squad car drove listlessly past the debris outside the flats to offer a presence, knowing that they could not deal with any disorder alone, that back up would take 15 minutes at least. The danger of being stabbed with an infected needle, or bitten by someone with HIV was not worth the bravery award. Little Meadows, Worsley, was the end of the line.

For his sins DI Mustoe was responsible for South Gloucester. At least Worsley was small enough to know most of the criminals. They tended to be the inconsequential petty thieves and burglars. Their shoplifting coincided with the twice daily buses, their burglaries only possible if they had access to stolen cars. It was not hard to work out who had done what to whom. Pinning it on them was neither easy nor worth the effort. It required surveillance for which there were no staff, evidence, and the introduction of the Police and Criminal Evidence legislation had rendered his previous successes by bullying unworkable and what for? They were as likely to get let off with a conditional discharge or Probation anyway. They were free to carry on doing it over and over again. The best he could offer was to assure people they were there, hence the nightly tour by the squad car, visits to the shopkeepers to remind them they could help if asked.

It was on one of these nightly patrols that the first body had been found. A young girl, not much more than 16, forced by withdrawal and desperation, having been unable to persuade any of the dealers to exchange sex for drugs had stumbled into a top floor flat in the tower block. The occupant, Paul Manners, a thirty something addict who did not deal, kept himself to himself and did not seem interested in screwing local girls, had lived there about six months. People knew he had things, possessions which was unusual for a scag head. A radio casette, music tapes and books. He could draw, when he had paper, and in summer he got extra money outside the cathedral doing portraits for tourists. The begging he saved for the winter. He had an appealing, sad, Christ like demeanour that drew the sympathy of passers-by and discouraged brutality from the police. He got his money, scored in Gloucester and caught the last bus back to Worsley each day to live in quiet isolation from all the dealings on the estate. He simply did not let any other users in.

Frankie, the sixteen year old, quite liked the look of him and tried to engage him in conversation on the bus home a couple of times. But he was too cerebral for her; unable to engage in the banter of the estate, the local gossip or talk about pop music. He was polite but aloof. In the anguish of her condition she thought he might take pity on her and might have something stashed away to make the cramps go away, stop the sickness and the feeling of spiders creeping under her skin.

When she had got to the door it was shut but there was a piece of frosted glass at one side where someone had smashed it to let themselves in. She could see through this hole that he was lying face down in front of the bathroom door. She was too young to realise he had been dead some days. Too scared to call the police she had gone down to the town, walking all the way in the dark, to sell herself to get money for drugs. She happened on one of the farm hands, who dabbled in most drugs and was not too fussy who he knocked up behind the pub after a few beers. He sobered up when she blurted out what she had seen. He had a good relationship with local police, handy if you needed to get back to the farm after too many jars. Many was the time he had been tanked up, stopped in the landrover by police and been warned and told to get off home. After all he would have no job without a license and the local police would not take that away from him. He would not meet anyone on the farm roads at night and the worst that could happen was he would drive into a ditch.

So he called the police and by midnight three police cars and a doctor had arrived at the flats. The doctor made a cursory examination of the festering sores in his arms and pronounced likely death from septicaemia. By 3am everyone was up and doing in Little Meadows. They all knew injecting drugs killed you if you got it wrong or bought bad gear but when you were clucking you would take a needle off a dead man. But everyone was surprised it was the quiet man from the top of the block. He was the one who collected clean needles, was organised, had a brain and used it, kept his own works, did not owe dealers; the last one they would expect to die.

It sent shock waves through the coherent few. A couple of users made up their minds to go into town and visit the counselling centre. One or two girls started enquiring of their doctors if they could get valium, which could blot out the cravings if you were not too addicted. Sales of cannabis went up, DF118S were exchanging hands at double the rate. The drug outreach workers saw it as a good opportunity to make some inroads on the estate. Alice and Colin, known to most of the residents already, started knocking on doors, handing out leaflets and talking to anyone who would let them in. Their primary message was safe use not drug treatment but the vain hope was always that, having befriended them, the users would seek treatment as well. But this only happened when their stealing and deception got them as far as prison and detox was mandatory. The pull of the drug was always stronger.

Today there was a second dead body. In two weeks that looked less like carelessness and more like crime. So DI Mustoe reluctantly put down the bun and listened to the sergeant.

"Looks like a regular scag head, 30s, made his money by dealing I'd guess so we don't see him much. Bit of driving and a couple of burglaries as a teenager but not much in the last five years. Local kids say he was a bit of a creep. Hangs around with 13 year olds, easy pickings for a dealer. Couldn't find anyone to admit he'd sold to them. He's where all the younger ones get their cannabis. A right fagin by the sound of it. No one wants to ID him though. I reckon that spate of thefts from cars after Christmas was down to him. Teaching the kids how to break in and selling them drugs in exchange for goods".

Mark Benson was four years in post and had just made sergeant. He thought Mustoe was a lazy, careless and second rate inspector and was not much pleased to be assigned to his team. Nevertheless he was not that good himself and he knew it. Only just scraped through his exams. It was only the shortage of recruits got him a promotion. Anyone with any promise headed up to the Mets or Avon. He had a new baby on the way and his wife, Janet, would not leave her parents now the baby was due. Leave it a couple of years, make a good effort where he was and if he was lucky he would get to Inspector one day and maybe into one of the other branches of the police that were springing up everywhere.

Benson agreed to meet Mustoe at the flats in fifteen minutes. Mustoe wolfed down the bun, swigged down with coffee and wearily shifted his bulk out of the chair, checked his radio and phone and collected some evidence logs and the kit he needed. Throwing them in the car he drove out on the long straight suburban roads of Gloucester through industrial estates, through farmland up the hills to the dull grey high street of Worsley. The shops were just opening, the cars parked on double yellow lines were ignored. Down the high street, left at the lights, drive for a mile and look for the signpost to the aerodrome. Mustoe could have found it in the dark, he had been there so many times before.

The bus stop was at the junction so the buses could turn round there. The first two rows were bungalows. Terraced, their white handrails along each path showing they were the vulnerable, glowed in the early morning light. Curtains twitched as they had all through dawn as the police cars had roared on to the estate. Here the paths were clean, the gardens neat, the buildings intact. Next, a small labyrinth of maisonettes, four stories high. Tidy on the outside but at night you could hear the rows, screaming women, angry men and frightened children. Outside, the grass, although cut, was strewn with paper, dirty nappies, bricks and debris and the overflowing bins had been dragged open by dogs and foxes. Old bicycle wheels, prams and a fridge were wedged into gaps behind the buildings. Not a soul in sight here. On turning left, right, left, the boarded up block of flats came into view and the concrete playground, its swings and roundabout smashed to pieces and every available surface swathed in graffitti. Mustoe noticed one or two youths walking in the direction of the flats turn towards him, make a reckoning and spit; but he had more important things to think about. The last block was swarming with police and residents, mainly teenage girls and children, who were cluttering up the area and distracting the officers.

"Get these people out of here, away from the scene" he shouted as he strode up to the first constable on guard. "They live here, Sir" said the constable who only looked sixteen himself. "Well persuade them to go inside and make themselves a cup of tea. We don't want the evidence going off on someone's shoe".

Evidence. For what? Another scag head on overdose? The chances of a crime having been committed was minimal - again. Why couldn't his patch have a stolen hoard of gold or government bonds found on it? A farm being used for drug production. IRA terrorists. A serial killer. Anything that would lift his daily grind into something of National importance and possible promotion. But no. Another junkie given up the ghost. They put on their paper suits on the landing and pocketed some masks and disinfectant swabs. DI Mustoe stepped over the threshold, took one breath and quickly stepped back again.

"Christ Almighty! What a stench!" He pulled out a handkerchief and sprinkled some antiseptic drops on it to cover his face. Dead bodies did not just smell they exuded a vapour that clung to your clothes, your hair and stuck in your throat. The flat had had all the windows open for about two hours but the smell was still unbreathable. The police photographer, looking green, was outside smoking a cigarette. Benson, with a surgical mask stuffed with cotton wool, was looking apoplectic round the outside of it, using a metal coat hanger to lift bits of clothing to inspect the damage. Mustoe made a cursory oversight of the room. Not your usual junkie then. There were posters on the wall, sci-fi mainly, Che Guevara, IRA pictures. Books in a cabinet, mysteries, UFOs that kind of thing. It was clear some built in cupboards had been ransacked, food, toiletries, bedlinen were all missing. No TV, radio or stereo but gaps where they might have been. The fridge door left open - empty.

"There's probably dozens been through here raiding the place since he died." He observed to Benson. Mustoe asked the photographer to come back and photo the empty cupboards and missing electrics. "No doubt there will be plenty of forensics in here."

"This could be blood poisoning or overdose but it could also be an infectious disease. We'd better warn the doctor," said Benson. The soccos were arriving now. In their white suits they looked like psychiatric nurses on a mission. If the soccos did their job they might get a burglary out of it.

Benson, braving the stench, had lifted aside the unbuttoned shirt of the corpse, revealing a T shirt with Iron Maiden on it. The putrefaction had seeped into it and, clutching his mask even tighter, Benson nudged the shirt to reveal the armpit. Jumping back he exclaimed "God Almighty. What's that?" he stammered. Mustoe turned his bulk to look, "Yeuch. What the hell do these people get up to?" he yelped.

In the armpit was a swelling as large as an egg, now black. On whisking the other side of the shirt it revealed another one in the other armpit. The neck, similarly, was blackened and swollen but the bluebottles had got there first, disturbing any silhouette the lump might have had. They both stared; repulsed but fascinated. Benson had seen a few dead bodies in his time but always felt as if it were his first, hence the precautionary masks and disinfectant he carried but this was far beyond anything he had witnessed before.

"Let's get some air, lad" Mustoe advised, trying not to breathe. He on the other hand had not witnessed as many bodies as Benson but thought he was inured to death as his father had run an abbatoir. As far as he was concerned once the life had gone out of a corpse it was just so much flesh. The deterioration and smell was part of life and death as much as any of the finer rituals were. As they emerged into light drizzle the forensic examiner appeared to pronounce death. "Where's Hargreaves?" said Mustoe without making polite introductions. The police doctor eyed him with distaste "Police thug" he thought. Dr David Champion was a crusader, not tainted with scepticism. He had moved from Oxfordshire to work in pathology and now was deputy Forensic Examiner to Dr Hargreaves, when he was on holiday.

"I'm David Champion. I will be doing all the forensic work while Dr Hargreaves is away." He said in a take it or leave it tone and looked straight into Mustoe's face. Mustoe smirked a bit and thought "you won't be so cocky lad when you've gone through that door." Benson, feeling more affinity for the younger man and embarrassed by his boss's attitude added "It's a bad sight and the smell is terrible, you will need to wear the mask, doctor." David Champion hesitated, he decided the young chap was trying to be helpful not deriding him so he thanked him and went up the stairs.

He stepped nimbly over the threshold, Mustoe following with a giant handkerchief over his face, and the three of them stared at the body. "First stage maggots; that means at least three days ago. The body is post rigor and temperature is the same as the room temperature. I pronounce death at 06.13 am on 5th June". The doctor then leaned closer to look at the neck sores. Benson moved his mask slightly to speak. "I think you should look at the armpits, doctor, there's something strange about this one".

Dr. Champion moved the shirt and peered as close as he dared. "Good Lord, I've never seen anything like that before. I'm really not sure what this is. It could be puncture wounds but I don't know how he would inject at that position or find a vein from that angle. Addicts do some peculiar things though. They usually go for the feet or the groin, or the neck if someone else is there to do it. But his arms don't look too bad. He must have taken some care to start with". He looked more closely at the neck. "He can't have punctured the artery or there would be blood all up the walls". Mustoe turned grey and put a strong mint in his mouth.

"So what are you suggesting, doctor, that someone messed with the body after he died?" Dr. Champion stood back and breathed out slowly. Then he noticed the hand, also infested with maggots. "It looks like his finger has been infected for some time. It's very swollen and the maggots appear to have started there first, see they are much larger than the others. It is possible these lesions are not injection sites but infection of the lymph glands." Mustoe looked at him straight. "Are we dealing with a contagious illness?" Dr Champion nodded. "I think until we can rule it out we had better treat this as notifiable. I won't be able to confirm until I get him back to the lab". The mortuary staff, looking anxious and sickened, in masks and suits, removed the body in a bag.

They all shuffled out of the building giving the constable instructions that anyone on that level should be seen by a doctor and no one else. No one was to leave or enter the building until a diagnosis was made, and that quarantine of the area was to begin immediately. Mustoe got on to HQ and spoke to his Governor alerting the contagion procedures to be instigated. "We'll need a lot of backup on this one" he growled, "to keep this lot from spreading disease everywhere."

Benson looked aside and tried to think of things to take his mind off what he had seen. Cotswold villages were meant to be golden and picturesque, falls of roses down their walls and overflowing cottage gardens and curious iron work peeping between the greenery. What had happened to Worsley was more like the centre of some Metropolis; concrete, grey and lifeless. Bitterness and depression oozing out of every pavement and building. A begrudging, mean spirited town, set in an unremarkable agricultural landscape.

Champion was frowning when he recovered his thoughts. "I can't see any injection sites. He is a mature man with several years' experience under his belt. They are usually quite good at medical practice. No sign of chaotic use, no needles lying around, more likely to take care, have a routine. It could be a reaction to something poisonous, contaminated drugs, but these lesions! If he had septicaemia he must have been ill for days."

"Septicaemia? That's what the other one died of," said Mustoe. "What other one?" asked Champion. "The last one Hargreaves did from here. Found in a flat upstairs with similar swellings and blackening. Didn't you see it?" Champion looked puzzled. "No I was away myself last month and we have so many bodies in and out. I don't expect Dr Hargreaves thought it was out of the ordinary." Now all three looked puzzled. Mustoe gathered his thoughts, "Is that usual for junkies, to die of septicaemia?" Champion answered. "Well yes, but they would usually start to feel ill then seek help. Often it's too late but we would see them before they died and get some history of what they were doing." Odd that these two were struck down so quickly they did not seek help from anyone, thought Mustoe. "You couldn't seek help round here if you were in trouble, rob you as soon as look at you. It is clear his flat's been turned over, probably more than once. I wouldn't put it past them to step over a dying man to get a stereo to flog." Champion frowned. "Surely they would call someone, even anonymously." Mustoe gave a wry smile. "This man is known locally as a fence and a pusher to kids. He'd have had a stash of drugs here, money as well likely, and stolen goods. Plenty to risk venturing over a dying body for. Someone had a motive to leave him to die and if they did it could be murder!"

Chapter Two

Suzannah

IT WAS HOT, thank the Lord. Suzannah stood barefoot at the casement window in the eaves; she wore a cotton chemise, most darned and mended, but it had belonged to the Mistress at Worsley Hall when her mother was there in service. One of the daughters of the squire had had it no doubt. Suzannah was used to hand-me downs. She had never had anything else, but then nor had her brothers or sisters or contemporaries in the town of Worsley. She looked into the apple trees of the orchard, the sun sparkling through the leaves at the little timber framed cottage and its deep thatched roof.

"I shall be one of the ladies and wear linen like this fresh made" she promised herself. It was not unheard of. One of the girls up Wooton way had married the Lord of the Manor after his wife died in childbirth; she was a labourer's daughter too, not like Suzannah whose grandfather was a smallholder. They kept chickens, two pigs and a cow and they had a maidservant of their own. Suzannah's grandfather had been a handsome man and caught the eye of a merchant's daughter in Bath. As a wool fuller he had no prospects but he had aspiration and was able to persuade the local wool merchant that his smart good looks and clever tongue would be an asset selling the product further afield and he agreed to go on commission to Bristow where he proved himself well worth his opinion.

By the age of thirty her Grandfather had built up quite a trade in west country ports and markets selling good cloth and employing three men as fullers as well as supporting two apprentices. He married a good steadfast woman and they had six children to bless them. Suzannah's father was the second youngest boy, not as smart and resourceful as his father but was able to go into the fulling business as an apprentice without paying his due and the family business flourished, supporting the two brothers and three sisters. Suzannah's father and next older brother kept the business going after two other brothers went to sea as commissioned officers. One was killed at sea and the other settled in Oxford having been made quite wealthy by their trade. Reuben Garrod retired at fifty, passing the business on to his eldest son and nephew and now lodged in this small cottage in the valley of the Evenlode. The families had lived here for centuries and Suzannah's mother had been lady's maid to Eliza Martyn now deceased and her son now Squire of the Hall.

Now Suzannah, their youngest daughter at fifteen, was to be taken into the service of his wife Rebecca Martyn. She was to be the companion of their daughters aged fourteen and ten and would learn manners and social niceties, dancing and fine sewing although Suzannah so far had not shown much propensity for these to date. Her mother,

Hannah, had a soft spot for young Suzannah. She just knew that once mixing with her betters she would make the most of their aspirations and come to good. Her eldest daughter Jane, had married a farmer's son and had her own estate now and her own maid. Her second daughter Constance was not so handsome but had done well to marry the baker in Tetbury and although it troubled her to have her daughter so far away, she did not sniff at the sacks of flour and grain that her daughter sent quarterly to the family. And now Constance was to be a mother too. Only Suzannah to be cleverly matched and all the girls were off her hands.

"Hurry up Suzannah and get you dressed" her mother called out from the floor below. It was not much past dawn and the household was bustling about already preparing to go to church. Suzannah was not much taken with domestic duties, having avoided them often enough when her sisters were around, but she was supposed to be hot pressing their linen and collars before church and had some mending on her bonnet to finish yet. She washed in the earthenware dish brought up by the servant, Mary, dried herself on a linen cloth and used an elm twig to clean her teeth. She appeared downstairs in her blue gown and black shoes although her knitted hose was darned several times over no one would see them.

"Put that iron in the fire, Mary," she ordered. She liked to give orders, "and bring the gruel to the table child" she added, knowing this would irritate Mary who was only a year younger than her. She ate her gruel and barley bread, washed down with ale, before she took the irons from the fire and began starching the white linen quoif for her mother's bonnet. She did the ribbons and a piece of lace before she had to swap the irons, using the starch water as her mother had shown her. When she had laid all the linen on chairs to dry she picked up her bonnet and set to mending the frayed edge neatly. "Oh Mother," she sighed as Hannah came through the kitchen door from the pantry. "I cannot wait to start service with Squire Martyn. I hear his daughter is such a sweet child and I shall grow up with her as a woman and will know all her secrets".

"Well child, what secrets could a fourteen year old, well born girl have? None of your scheming ideas I should think. They will have a husband lined up for her already, I should think, with their connections." Suzannah wrinkled her brow. "What Mother, should she not fall in love first?" "With all their wealth? Go on girl, she must be well matched to favour their family, not please herself." Hannah put her hands on her hips. She felt Suzannah was far less sensible than her other daughters and wondered if letting her out of the home was a good idea after all. "I would not be surprised if she were not betrothed to the Berkeleys somewhere along the line, a second son or cousin or something". Her mother sat to contemplate. "I hear Squire Martyn has bought two more corvettes that sail to the West Indies and back, slaves there to Virginia and spices and sugar back. My but he will be rich one day with the trade protected from piracy these days."

"What are slaves Mother?" Suzannah asked guilelessly. "They are heathen men, who know no Godliness that are black as father's hat. When I once travelled to Bristow with your father we saw them unloaded at the dock. Such a pain to my heart to see their suffering, chained foot to foot and in such misery. Nevertheless they will be taught God's way when they reach their destination. Hard work and prayer will make them thankful for being saved".

Suzannah could not imagine how these men had allowed themselves to be enslaved, but supposed that anyone who did not live their lives through God must inevitably suffer. She crossed her heart and made a little prayer that she, Suzannah, should never be beholden to any man or master other than her father or husband.

And that was the crux of it. How to find a good husband. Although Suzannah was only fifteen she was a strapping girl having access to milk and cheese as a babe and not weaned until a year old by her doting mother. She had fine teeth and fair freckled skin that she had to hide from the sun at all times, rich blond curls and breasts like fine apples. In her finery she guessed there was no other maid in the village more handsome. She had some suitors. The smith's son, all muscles and hairy forearms, was always doffing his hat in her direction, the curate, so weak and pale, had more than once indicated his wishes from afar and her uncle's wool seller was also paying compliments to her whenever she visited her aunt in the village. But Suzannah believed she was meant for better things. She would have a gentleman's son, with a private income and where better to meet one than up at the Hall.

It was now June and she was due to start there on midsummer's day. She tied her shoes and bonnet on, found her lawn gloves and by 7.30 am was walking with her mother, Mary, and behind them, her father and John the manservant. They made their way down the lane towards the centre of the town where the great stone church with its new bell tower rang out the call to mass. Church services were long and boring and Suzannah spent much of the sermon teasing the curate by narrowing her eyes and showing her teeth as he was assisting the priest and trying to see what ribbons and lace Miss Martyn was wearing. "Oh I should look so much finer in those new clothes" thought Suzannah, "than that skinny little Madam."

Maria Martyn was thirteen and a half just younger than Suzannah and was as dark as Suzannah was fair. She had deep brown eyes and glossy hair that was caught up in a snood beneath her cap. She wore fine leather gloves and laced up leather shoes with heels. The lace on her collar, splayed over her shoulders, was far too exotic for church thought Suzannah. It must be Spanish or Flemish. Now her father owned shipping she would be clothed in every garment the East and West Indies could provide no doubt. Suzannah had no idea what the West Indies was but supposed it supplied riches and finery. Once out of church Suzannah's mother pushed her to the fore as the Martyns left, talking to the minister.

"Good morrow Hannah" Martyn doffed his hat slightly "Is this the new maid to our household? Here Maria, Suzannah will soon be joining us to be your companion and mistress in waiting. I hope you will be devout sisters." Suzannah made a deep curtsey, "with respect sir it will be a great honour you do me, to allow me service in your household and I am right conscious of the graciousness of your offer." He gloated at her. "How charming. We will send for you in ten days when my wife is stronger and able to welcome you to our household."

Suzannah was all too aware why Squire Martyn's wife was unable to come to church, or go out in society at present.

She had had two miscarriages in the last year and it was said he made very great demands on her in that sense. Mistress Martyn's seamstress lived in the next village and said she often locked her chamber against him and it caused very bad feeling in the house. They had two daughters aged thirteen and ten and a boy aged eight but Squire Martyn had a mind to produce more sons to inherit his business and wealth. Rebecca Martyn was a shadow of her former self. She married his good looks and he married her money but once the flash of passion died there was little between them. Squire Martyn was always away from home on one business concern or another and word had it that he had a mistress in Bristow with one child of his already.

Suzannah looked up at him through her eyelashes and did not miss the sly, lecherous appraisal he gave her. She thought it might offer her a lot of amusement in the months to come. Ten days later, with a chest of clothes and her toilette, she was conveyed by cart to Worsley Hall; its stone façade and porticoed doorway seemed to suck her in like a mouth. The square hall was stone flagged and still had a live fire burning but felt chill and dark all the same. The oriel window above the door was a good thirty feet above and had engraved coats of arms in the glass in jewel like colours. Rebecca Martyn, the Squire's wife, sat in an oak chair, her two daughters flanking her like a cloak and a woman in severe puritan clothes beside her. This was Ann Friend her housekeeper. She would be in charge of the lady's maids and looked fierce. Suzannah curtseyed and lowered her eyes, demurely.

"Welcome Suzannah. We hope you will prosper in our household and we look to you to befriend and protect our children, Maria and Catherine, and care for them as one of our family." Suzannah curtseyed again. She thought one curtsey was enough for two girls. There was no sign of Squire Martyn today.

"Come with me," commanded Ann Friend, marching towards a corridor at the rear of the hall; from there a narrow staircase wound up to the first floor where she was shown a great chamber with a window, all glass, facing east. She was to sleep in the same bed as Maria and it did look luxurious, its woven bed curtains thick and warm, its linen sheets crisp and clean. There were fresh and dried flowers in bowls about the room and a great linen press full of folded garments in fine lawn and lisle.

"You will be expected to prepare all Miss Maria's clothes and dress her. I will show you to start with and you must learn. She has her hair dressed every morning and you will be responsible for that too. The under maid will bring water and toiletting articles to this chamber in the morning. You are not to use the soaps and perfumes. They are for Miss Maria's sole use. Nor are you to wear any of her under garments, accoutrements, jewellery or hair pins. Do you understand?"

Suzannah nodded. She noticed there were three doors in this room. The door from the back stairs up which she came, hidden in the panelling and a grand oak door to the central staircase over the hall. A further door to one side led to another room. "That is the closet. You may use a separate convenience to Miss Maria and the servants will change the pots as necessary." Susannah peeped inside. There was a shelf at the back with a metallic screen she could see her face in, and combs and brushes laid out on lace cloths.

There was a low cupboard in which there were small doors behind which the china chamber pots were kept once used. Susannah was pleased to see they would have some privacy. She had been used to sharing bedrooms with her sisters but Maria was a stranger to her.

"May I know where to store my gown Mistress?" Ann Friend showed her a cupboard built between the walls of Maria's bedroom and the next room There were hanging hooks there and a chest for smaller items. The Butler brought up Suzannah's trunk and pushed it roughly in beside the other.

"You'd better get downstairs where you are wanted girl" he barked at her. "I am Suzannah to you and I beg you to tell me how I shall call you, brother?" "Cowle is my name but you may call how you find me if we get to know each other better!" He winked lewdly at her behind Ann's back. Suzannah felt indignant. She had come here to be admired by her betters not by the servants. What cheek. She kept her temper as she did not know the hierarchy of the household but thought she might get her revenge soon enough. She followed Ann down the back stairs.

"You may use the main staircase when you accompany Maria. At all other times you will use the servant's staircase. Do you understand?" Suzannah wondered if she thought her simple. "Of course mistress."

Suzannah was already beginning to see how complicated this could be. She would sleep with Maria, appear in public with her and be accessible to her most intimate activities but at all other times she must be denoted by lower rank, not even allowed free use of the stairs. She went back down the servant's staircase and joined Maria and Rebecca in the hall where Maria was practicing on a spinette. "Would you like me to show you?" said Maria.

"Very much" replied Suzannah obediently. No doubt playing an instrument would be a great advantage to her future rise up the social ladder. Maria showed her how to stretch her fingers and press the keys making a rich twanging note almost like a harp. Suzannah tried and tried until they both laughed at her difficulty. Rebecca Martyn ignored them. She sat immediately next to the fire, a wool cloak around her skirts, embroidering her sampler. Ann Friend sat opposite, sorting threads, winding them and passing them to her mistress. They did not speak. Catherine sat on a rug playing rhinestones and talking to her doll. It was a strange, formal place to spend one's time and compared to Suzannah's cheerful, chatty home with five children all talking at once. Here it felt like they were being punished.

The water clock in the hall struck twelve and the family rose for dinner. They filed into the dining hall, the table being laid with pewter and silver. Before sitting they kneeled beside the table and said Grace, Rebecca leading and the household responding. Suzannah sat up in a carved chair and looked at the cutlery. At home they had spoons for broth and gruel and mother cut the meat and cake with a knife and put it on their wooden platters. Here the servants put the food on her plate and she had her own knife to cut it with. There was pheasant, dumpling, gravy and greens, a savoury tart, aspics and a spiced pudding with fruit syrup. Suzannah had never eaten such food even in the festivals at Christmas and Easter. She ate little, believing that delicate ladies should not be seen gorging themselves, however tasty the food. She was pleased to note all the ladies ate like that,

Rebecca eating even less than Maria. Daniel, the only male at table stabbed at his plate with his knife enjoying the scowls of Ann Friend. After Grace they ate in silence. There were no men present except Cowle who served the food and took away the dishes. The girls were given weak ale to drink and the women had diluted wine.

After dinner Maria asked her mother's permission to show Suzannah the grounds and they went out into a meadow where sheep grazed and beyond were two fine horses.

"My father has six horses for the carriage and two riding horses at present. We keep other horses for the farm but they are stabled by the byres. Walsh sees to all the horses. I have my own pony and so does Catherine, but you may ride if Catherine does not wish to go out."

Maria explained to her the routine of the day. In the mornings they had a tutor, a French Huguenot that came from the next parish. He taught them Latin and testaments. Her brother had learned Greek but her father did not think it necessary for the girls. After a walk in the fresh air they did sewing until dinner at twelve. Miss Friend taught embroidery and tapestry. In the afternoons they could walk or ride out if the weather was fine enough or if wet they could play in the hall or practice dancing. They were encouraged to go out in the fresh air as much as possible. After their exercise Maria had to practice the spinette for an hour, Catherine would learn but had a recorder at present. From then until daylight failed they were encouraged to read, usually from the bible or classics but sometimes poetry and the words to songs. They could sing while Rebecca played the spinette.

At six o'clock they went to their rooms. Miss Friend expected them to be abed by seven although frequently now Maria had been allowed to stay downstairs to be introduced to guests coming to dinner.

"Father has so many guests these days" sighed Maria. "He has to invite people from Gloucester and Bristow now he has so many ships." Suzannah brightened at this. In a year or two Maria would be able to join them at the supper table along with her companion; Suzannah would have access to all manner of wealthy and diverse businessmen and ship owners. She could hardly wait. She decided her task was to make herself the perfect companion for Maria, a solace to her mother and a delight to their master.

Maria's brother, heir to the Martyn fortune was eight years old. When he came to Rebecca she doted on him, hugging him tight and primping his dark curls. He did not like it and struggled to get away from her. Already his duty as a son and man had been impressed on him by his father. Daniel Martyn was already flaunted at dinner by his father; he encouraged his taste for wine and made him witness to the men and their bawdy ways. However Rebecca spoiled him Martyn knew these favours would put a wedge between her and Daniel and bind the child to his manly ways. Squire Martyn was not having his son and heir a weakly milksop brought up by women. Daniel already had his own tutor and was encouraged to think himself as superior to his sisters. Catherine thought he was the most admirable brother a child could want and to encourage her alliance, at least in public, he played with and courted her. In private he had already begun to denigrate and bully his mother and gave his sisters orders in which his mother supported him.

"Go to the end of the long room and fetch my spinning top" he would command and Catherine would submissively run to do his errand. "No I have changed my mind. Go and fetch my hoop and stick," he would snigger, as he watched her run again the length of the long gallery." She would run to meet his demands and he would copy his father, "you are a good child, now here is a groat," he would say magnanimously.

Maria, six years his senior, knew just how cruel he could be. She had already learned not to disclose her wishes knowing that he would do all to thwart her. If she chose to walk he would announce to the servant that the paths were too wet and she should stay indoors. If she chose to ride he would say the horse was lame, he had seen it with his own eyes and needed to go to the smith. Either Maria did not state her wishes in his presence or gave false counsel.

"I think I shall stay indoors and read my latin text" soon got Daniel out of her way. Then she could walk or ride at will. She was so glad for her new companion, who looked clever and willing and guessed she would not let Daniel get the better of her and with the two together he would surely be kept in his place.

The next day after dinner Maria had said "we shall go to the study and I will show you the atlas, Suzannah". Once in the study she confided in Suzannah how their plans should be made. "Daniel will go with Cowle to the stable and ride out or he will have a fencing lesson with his tutor, Benoit," she giggled. "then we can go out into the park. You will be my chaperone instead of mother or Ann and we shall have such fun." They waited twenty minutes and saw the water clock at the half hour. Then they stepped down the staircase and approached Rebecca.

"Mother, I should like to take the air and show Suzannah the park meadows and my pony. Pray may I?" Rebecca gave her a haunted look and consented.

"Be sure you do not go beyond the park boundary and do not speak to anyone that is not of our household," said Ann Friend. They curtseyed, but once out of the great oak door giggled and ran to the rear of the hall. Beside the house was a garden all yew hedges and secret places; Suzannah wanted to stop and look but Maria pulled her. At the back of the house was a cobbled yard where the carriages were stabled in barns. Two were empty.

"Where is your father Maria?" "Oh he has gone to Bristow, he is always there, his business takes him away, sometimes weeks at a time. Last year he went on the Mermaid to Barbados. He was away for months. He brought me back a music box all covered with shells from the Caribbean seas. I shall show you tonight".

Suzannah was pensive. She wondered how she would meet all these new people if Squire Martyn was always away. At least he would not go to the Caribbean again in two years. "My mother told me your father makes his money from selling slaves. Does he?" Maria was not perplexed. "Indeed he does. He is very good at picking those who are strong and will last the sea trip. And he instils in them God's word. On the boat he makes them pray daily for God's forgiveness".

"Forgiveness for what?" Suzannah questioned. "For practising diabolic ways in Africa. Father says he cannot tell what dreadful things they do in their homeland, it is too horrible, but they pray to the devil and worship him with the blood of animals. Father says he is saving them from eternal damnation by providing them with work and showing them the ways of the Lord".

Suzannah was quiet. She could not grasp how a whole nation of people could all be wrong and Squire Martyn right. He was not a Godly man at all, she could tell from his leering and suggestive manner to herself and the evidence of his miserable wife. A Godly man would seek to make his family happy and secure. He was a hypocrite no less. Suzannah began to plot how she would, in subtle ways, humiliate such a man. But there was time for that.

Here were the ponies. Maria climbed the wooden gate and called her pony. A smart grey welsh pony busily made its way to the gate followed by a smaller grey mountain pony rather too fat.

"This is Pendragon, my pony. He must not have too many apples, but I am allowed to give him one a day." She produced a red apple from her pocket in her pinafore and proceeded to bite off pieces to give to the ponies. She gave Suzannah a chunk to feed the other. They patted the ponies and agreed to ride out the next day if it was still fine and <u>not</u> tell Daniel.

Suzannah liked her charge. A conspiracy was just what she needed to keep herself amused. The stable boy came out to peer at them, a doltish youth with a hank of yellow hair in his eyes. Suzannah knew at fourteen she was beginning the peak of her allure and to a simple farm hand she would appear stunning, but now she was a lady's maid the farm hands had no right to stare at her like they did the milk maids who tarried and bantered with them. She was someone important now and meant to make the most of it.

Chapter Three

Stonefield

ROSE COLLINS STOOD at her flat window, a hand pulling distractedly at her fair hair, watching the police come and go in the block opposite. There were things she knew, things she could tell them that she was not going to. Older than most of the residents she had grown up in Worsley. Her father was a farm worker who abused her and her mother. Her mother he beat, her he used for sex. By the age of fifteen she had finally escaped to Gloucester with a lad from a travelling family. She stayed in a hostel for a few months, care of Social Services, then went off travelling with his family. Then she had got pregnant. Before long he had found someone else but he maintained the right to keep her beside him at first by bullying, then by beating. At seventeen with a year old child, absent partner and living in his mother's van she decided anything would be better. Finding a leaflet for Women's Aid in the doctors surgery and nothing to lose she had got into a refuge in Birmingham. He had found her, beat her, the police were called and the baby taken away. As it was only a domestic no charges were brought against him.

Deep down she found some strong willpower that kept her fighting back. She kept on at Social Services to let her have a flat, have her child back and was re-housed In Gloucester with her son and after three years she had dragged herself back to normality and swapped a house in Gloucester for a flat in Worsley. Her father was now dead and she could see her mother whenever she wanted. Her older sister lived in Gloucester and she thought life could be worse. She was her own boss as long as she could survive on benefits. Through her mother she had got a couple of cleaning jobs on the side which meant she could just manage the bills with a growing son. Danny was now ten years old. Stubborn, like her, defiant and old for his age. She had avoided the drug trap. It never interested her because she wanted to do it on her own without the help of professionals and medication.

They had never helped her so why should she help them now? But deep down she was worried. All Danny's school friends were getting into trouble. There was nothing for kids in Worsley and although the bus came for the older children to get to school in Gloucester, by 3.30pm they were back home trashing the playground, emptying the bins, scrawling on any surface. Even the youth centre was only open once a week for three hours. But Danny was not interested in that. He was not a joiner, he was a leader. You could see it in the playground; he called the shots, organised the others into games, meted out punishment. She did not like it but nothing she said had any effect. He was his father's son.

Despite that he did have a heart, especially for his mother. There had always been just the two of them, pitting their wits against the world. He would always defend her but she gave him no reason to. She was tough. She had learned tough from when she was not much older than him. You did not give people a chance to get inside your head or your heart. She had the odd relationship, comfort more than passion. Danny could not recall his father at all and she had explained openly why she had left him. Danny regretted not having a dad but so few of the other boys had a dad either and lots of theirs' were violent too, or drug users, or just wasters. He did not want a dad who was a waster; he had to be a hero. So the council worker who came to replace her windows was around for a couple of years, her cousins' mate she met in the pub stayed over for a year or so but they were not dad material as far as Danny was concerned.

John Freeman was a different case. Known as Jake he presented as quite a romantic character to the children of Little Meadows. He knew about everything. About bands because he had been a roadie for a band in the 70s- about UFOs and ghosts, about drugs and alternative lifestyles-he had lived in a peace camp for a while. He could get anything you wanted, but did not seem to be like the other druggies, pathetic and needy. All the boys at Danny's school liked being seen with Jake. Professionals might have been suspicious of his motives but what Jake got out of kids was information. Whose granny had stuff worth stealing, where she kept the spare key in the shed, who's Mum worked at some big house in the Cotswolds and would tell when the owners were away or when the housekeeper went out. Horses that were not micro chipped, who had pedigree dogs for stealing, people who left unsecured hanging baskets outside or shrubs in pots. Anything that could be stolen Jake knew about it and he sold the information in pubs in Gloucester. This was how he paid for his drugs and did not get caught by the police. Soon he found he knew enough about people that he could threaten blackmail in a small way. Not grass them up to the police of course but everyone had crossed someone in their time.

Eventually he retreated to Worsley as the situation in Gloucester got a bit too hot for him. He had passed some info to a gang of pushers about a runner who had cheated on them. They retaliated but the victim's brother heard Jake had been the cause and he gathered a posse of violent mates who sought him out. Time for Jake to make himself scarce. He had set himself up in Worsley within a month. One or two local lads with too much money and nothing to spend it on except beer were willing to experiment with any new drug going and he fleeced them with any pills he got his hands on. Some of his previous customers in Gloucester were still keen to get information about houses in the Cotswolds. Jake could keep watch on people's routines without attracting attention. He portrayed himself as an affable hippy in the village, chatting up shop keepers and publicans and never in trouble with the police.

He looked weird, long black hair, tattoos and recently his Freddy Mercury moustache, but appeared harmless. The parents did not see him hanging around with their kids at the bus stop, the playground or the old aerodrome so did not view him as dangerous. And the kids never said anything. Jake was great story teller. After school, teas eaten, homework ignored, the kids in droves wandered aimlessly about, tentatively sharing a cigarette, eyeing up the opposite sex, voicing their hopes and dreams. One of their attractions was Ron Beeney who kept a couple of old motorbikes in a shed at the back of his house and sometimes let them dismantle them then grease them and put them back together. Then there was Marj McCormack who was an alcoholic with a penchant for young boys. It was seen as a rite of passage to have slept with Marj when you were thirteen or fourteen and she let you watch as well, sometimes up to two or three boys all got into bed with her. A bottle of rough cider sweetened her up no end.

Then there was the Bunker. Not everyone was allowed in there. No one was in charge but if certain people were there, Jake being the main one, you had to be invited in. Usually dope was smoked, rough cider drunk and heroin on occasions smoked. No one told, so the police were unaware of it. It had been built in the second-world war when the aerodrome was a secondary landing space beyond Brize Norton. Planes had taken off from the Worsley aerodrome to bomb Germany so it was a target for bombing itself. The bunker was made of reinforced concrete round the back of the old hangar and right underground. It was about 15 feet long and six feet wide and could sit about 20 at a pinch. It showed as a slightly raised bump overgrown with hawthorn and brambles which disguised it fully from the air and the ground. After the war the aerodrome was abandoned and before the estate was built the airforce had sealed up the entrance with a metal door, bolted into the frame. Over the years a hole had been excavated next to the door that eventually the frame became exposed and a few sledge hammer blows had dislodged the door enough to get in.

Beyond the door the floor dropped down about four feet and a metal rung ladder, now rusted away, had gone down inside the door. Over the years water penetration and earth movements had cracked the walls so that soil from outside spilled into the back of the room. The walls were covered in daubs and pornography. If people came they sat on old crates with rags on, a deck chair and a few old car seats. It smelled and was damp but its dereliction suited the hopelessness of youth and its secrecy was its attraction. During about three generations it had developed a sort of taboo. People like Ron Beeney knew about it but never went there, viewing it as a den of thieves and criminals with whom he did not wish to associate. Others who had briefly visited gained the idea it was haunted, with dead airmen (according to Jake), small children heard about it and instinctively knew not to talk about it. It was a man's place, no girls were invited, and no one mentioned it in passing. Stories were told there, drugs were swapped and tried out, people passed out on alcohol, plans for burglaries were hatched. All the people who used it had a vested interest in keeping quiet.

Rose's Danny was just too young to be able to go but he knew all about it. Jake had said he could go "when he was a man" and Danny was determined he would be that by the age of twelve. At least, Danny was not sure what constituted being a man but it was something to do with sex and drugs and taking risks. Danny's neighbour, Billy Smith, had a picture of himself being given a blow job by Marj McCormack. It was a polaroid and so well handled the picture was all crinkled up now. Billy said they had to get her drunk so she would not notice or she would have taken it off them. Billy had only been thirteen as he had had the picture two years now. Billy was a regular at the bunker and he smoked cannabis when he could get the money together. This involved stealing small amounts from his mother's purse which she did not seem to miss and mildly blackmailing her boyfriend, who was married. Billy did not say but gently hinted that Roy, the boyfriend, would be in trouble if his wife, who owned a plant centre in the next village, found out. Roy, foolishly, often gave Billy a ten pound note without telling his mother, assuming Billy would use it to go to the cinema or buy model aeroplanes with it. Roy had more money than sense.

Danny wondered how you got in to see Marj. You had to keep your mouth shut more than anything. No one wanted her stopping her hobby because some interfering police man or social worker got wind. Secrecy was the key word to all rites of passage. You must not let your Dad know you smoked cigarettes; you did not tell your girlfriend about Marj; you did not let your Mum smell your breath if you had been up the rec with a gallon of rough cider. Drugs had their own language so that outsiders did not know what you were talking about. It was a wonderful fantasy world that only special people could join in and that definitely excluded parents. Danny intended being one of the gang.

Rose was not naïve. She could see the temptation for a ten year old boy on this estate. She had told him all about drugs, already seen the dangers, not far from the school gates. The older boys who hung about with younger ones, the ones who visited "uncles" in Gloucester, who were popular, who were like magnets to other boys. She did not know if they had drugs or pornography or what but it was never too early to warn sons about the consequences of these things. Sex however had not crossed her mind. She still saw Danny as a child, easily tempted but not sexually active for two or three years and, although she knew about Marj McCormack (dirty cow), she did not think she was a threat to Danny, not yet anyway. Grown-ups having sex with children had been part of her life too. It was not any use telling the authorities. They did not stop it happening just moved it around a bit so you ended up in a home being abused by strangers or in a home full of disturbed teenagers who did the same to you.

Now Rose stood and watched the police go in and out of the flats, white paper suits, the big fat one she recognised as in charge; the doctor in a brown jacket with his bag and now the police undertakers with the body bag and a stretcher. Of course she knew Jake was dead. She had known before the police. Who had said? She could not remember. At five am she had got up with a headache, hearing shouting outside. Tina from next door was on the pavement in a dressing gown looking scared and two youths were talking excitedly to her and pointing to the flats across the road. Rose had opened the window and called out "What's going on?" Tina had said "They've found Jake dead, in his flat. She hadn't recognised the boys, was not sure if Tina was referring to them or not. Someone had called the police and by 8am the place was crawling with them; cars, vans sirens, lights. "What for?" she asked herself; they were not coming to save anyone's life were they.

What surprised her was Danny's reaction. He had got up when she called out to Tina, asked what was happening and when she said "Jake Freeman's dead" she was sure there were tears in Danny's eyes. She was shocked. She did not think Danny knew him more than to nod to. She would wait till things quietened down a bit and then ask him how well he knew him. Jake Freeman was a slime ball as far as she was concerned, a poser, full of rubbish tales that no one believed. He had worked with Black Sabbath, then it was Led Zeppelin, then Deep Purple. Every time the story changed. He was a waste of space. He had appeared from Gloucester about two years ago, clearly out of desperation, no connections with Worsley, and settled in quickly enough. Who was she to judge him though? She knew he hung out with younger boys but not ten year olds. She thought he was just immature, no one said he was gay. He had a girlfriend he toted round the pubs occasionally. He could get you cheap gear for cash. He had offered to lend her money at 30% for the month. She had shied clear of him since. She was afraid one day she would be so desperate she would need a loan shark, if the washer broke down or she could not pay the electric bill in winter or her Mum died. Always she lived with the fear she would one day be that desperate.

She did two cleaning jobs, one for her aunt's friend who had a big house near Cirencester. It was only £3 an hour but it was a big house and she could spin it out and it was regular, no questions asked. Maureen sent a car to collect her as well although she had to get the bus back. It was £9 a week less bus fare and Maureen was lonely and kind. On her cleaning days she would have coffee and biscuits; real coffee and chocolate biscuits; and Maureen would talk about her life before widowhood, before grief. Rose harboured a dream that when Danny was older Maureen would become frail and ask her to move in to look after her. She fancied living in a big house with no neighbours and no noise outside. She did not mind a bit of nursing, she could cook and Maureen seemed to like her, but they were miles apart classwise. Her other job was cleaning one of the pubs in the high street, the best one. It was up the far end of the town and she had to walk the mile or so there, but it was nice inside, with log fires and copper to polish. It was the only pub that had window boxes in summer and did proper food in the day, not just cheese rolls and crisps. She had a ripe imagination did Rose. She saw herself being entertained there by an old sugar daddy with a Jaguar, buying her a three course lunch with wine and not having to go back to the estate and provide three teas for her and Danny for £2.50. Beans on toast, cheese and potato pie, tinned spaghetti. Week in, week out, the same thing.

But she was not desperate. Not yet. Her mother had bought Danny a whole set of clothes for his birthday, good stuff, and her aunt had promised him designer trainers this summer. Her sister had bought him a skate board and she had got him a second hand stereo tape system from the bloke in the pub. Not even knocked off. Rose gained some pride from the fact she never got bent gear, never used drugs, and never sold her body to get money. All those things were unusual amongst her acquaintance. She did not bang on about it just quietly contemplated it and it was the source of her self- respect. She hoped that Danny had absorbed the same feeling but here he was crying over some scumbag dealer.

She turned away from the window wondering if she should go to the police about Jake. She knew he was a drug user, everyone knew that but not heroin, he definitely did not look like a user. Did they know he befriended young boys? Maybe this was a murder, someone he had crossed in Gloucester or he had touched someone up and the father had killed him. Had he done anything to Danny? She started to fret. She could not feel safe until she had spoken to him but now was not the right time.

After she got Danny off to school, washed and dressed, she had to go up to the pub to clean from ten to eleven thirty, so on her return there was just the one police constable outside the flats. The red and white tape shimmered in the damp breeze and he looked fed up. She stopped for a chat but he was non-committal about what had happened to Jake. Was it secret? Was there something suspicious? She decided to call on Tina and find out what the locals knew. Tina was a slut. She did not even clean the house unless social services were coming round and she had four children all at awkward ages. A baby still in nappies, a fractious three year old at home and an eight year old boy friendly with Danny and a fourteen year old daughter it was thought was on the game. Other than that Tina was kind hearted and liked a gossip. She had helped out Rose when her family were not there for her.

Tina said that one of the boys she had been speaking to that morning had been at another flat about 4am watching videos. They had been drinking and there was a row. He was friendly with Chantal, Tina's daughter. On leaving the block the lad had wandered up to Jake's corridor and found the door open, realising he was long dead. Unlike the locals who had seen it as an opportunity to loot everything he had, this boy had had been sick then sought sanctuary at Tina's and told her what he had seen. Tina had waited an hour or so then about 5.30am decided to call the police; if only to stop the rotting corpse infecting the rest of the flats. By 6.30am everyone knew Jake was dead. Many had known a couple of days but had said nothing. That new radio or video, the three new shirts or packet of razors had come from Gloucester not Jake Freeman's flat. Almost everyone had a bit of the spoils so no one was talking to the police. Rose tentatively asked Tina what Jake got up to with the boys who hung around him and was not surprised to hear he gave them cannabis and showed them pornography. Nor was she surprised he coached them in shoplifting, burglary and snooping on others. Tina smoked cannabis anyway so she did not think it as anything to worry about. If Chantal got a bit of a puff it did not do her any harm, did it? She was not worried Jake would supply hard drugs. He did not use them and she seemed to think he had a strong sense of morality where heroin was concerned. Apparently it was due to what he had seen it do the rock stars he had fraternised with in the past.

Despite being a school day Chantal was indoors hanging around having only got up at lunchtime. "It's the curse," explained Tina, "She always gets the cramps. Can't go to school like that". Chantal looked remarkably calm for someone supposedly in pain. While Tina went to make tea Rose casually asked her if she had hung out with Jake Freeman after school. Chantal informed her that she would rather die than be seen with him but he was only interested in boys and they went somewhere secret to smoke dope. She was not sure where but supposed it was someone's flat. Maybe it was in the village? She knew they used all sorts of drugs because the boys bragged about it at school but not hard drugs. She could not say if sex was an attraction. No one said anything like that. Jake was not a ponce, if anything the boys admired his style, but only the young ones.

Rose came away feeling she had learned nothing more than she already knew but less anxious that Danny had been abused by him. She would make the cheese and potato pie and get some chocolate biscuits and talk to Danny after school.

Chapter Four
Squire Martyn

AFTER SUZANNAH HAD been at the Hall for three weeks Squire Martyn returned. He came at seven in the evening in a great flurry of carriage horses and postilions, all leaping to his assistance. His family stood before the doorway to greet him, with Suzannah behind them, looking demure. He shouted a great deal, much as the farm lads did after drinking too much ale, and she saw the postilion push some bottles under a seat in the carriage as he stepped down. He ignored Rebecca but held out his arms to Daniel who bowed formally, then pestered to know what gifts his father had brought him. Squire Martyn acknowledged his daughters and asked his wife if all was well in the home, to which she assented with one word. The family all moved indoors with Suzannah and Anne Friend behind and the postilion brought in two chests from the carriage. From one Squire Martyn drew out a perfect model of a gallion with all the gunwales open and tiny guns peeping out.

"Here's what we see off the Spaniards with," he roared, making exploding noises which Daniel copied. Rebecca winced.

"And here for my little duchess" he said, turning to Maria, "is a fine garment for your wardrobe". He produced a beautiful lace mantilla with jet combs to hold it in place. Maria was delighted and flung her arms about his neck. "Oh Papa you are so kind to me." For Catherine a wooden puppet on strings and for Rebecca a fine black shawl. Rebecca responded politely but reservedly. "Indeed you are a generous husband." She kissed him briefly on his cheek but Suzannah noticed she closed her eyes in disgust as she did so.

Suzannah did not expect a gift but felt wistful that her station in life meant she was never led to expect anything. Perhaps one day she would have a husband who would bring her fine lace and shawls. She had only to wait and be clever. As Squire Martyn proceeded into the dining hall, calling for porter, she smelt the sour wave of alcohol on his breath and as he was turning to instruct the servants to put away the chests immediately Suzannah had to pass by him through the doorway. She was the last through and suddenly felt the weight of something at the back of her skirt. She wore a stiff petticoat, her skirts were copious but she still felt the pressure through the folds. Squire Martyn had put his hand upon her rump. She prevented herself from turning around but moved forward quickly and blushed furiously. The light was fading and she turned towards the fire where the glow would disguise her embarrassment. However when she had the courage to look up Squire Martyn was staring straight at her and smirked when he caught her eye. She had to think how to deal with this situation and get the upper hand and hiding her discomposure was the first measure so she looked brazenly and haughtily back at the Squire as if she was goosed by a titled man every day of the week.

"And how is our new servant progressing?" he asked Rebecca looking intently at Suzannah.

"Suzannah has proved a devout and sensible companion to Maria. She is well versed in Latin and texts and has come on a little at the spinette. Maria is well turned out daily and Suzannah has a tidy way with her coiffure and attire which brings out Maria's finer points. We are well pleased with her so far." Squire Martyn looked pleased. Pretty and useful he thought. He had made a good judgement there and now he had six weeks to admire her at close quarters.

The children were sent up to bed and the nearest neighbours, land owners, came to dine. Suzannah pretended to go to sleep but lay awake trying to imagine what fine glasses and cutlery and silver would be on the table. She had glimpsed the kitchen cook making game jellies and custards flavoured with angelica and rosewater. Thomas the gardener had been busy all morning digging potatoes and greens and taking up the saladings and up his ladder in the orchard collecting sweet peas for the table. She fell asleep to dreams of a grand ball where she was dancing, dancing and wearing a fine silk gown and mantilla.

The next day Suzannah and Maria were at lessons when they heard a commotion in the hall. Squire Martyn was in a temper. He said harsh words to Rebecca, announced he would be out all day, visiting neighbours, and she was to "put her house in order by his return."

Their tutor closed the door to the hall and Suzannah wondered what was wrong with the household that he should be so aggravated by it. She had grown up in a God-fearing household where early rising and hard work was the order of the day and she had not close knowledge of a drunkard in the house.

In carrying for Maria Suzannah had to use the servant's stair. This came out by the kitchen and house-keeper's parlour. The kitchen drudge slept in the room on a pallet and by five a.m. was up stoking the great fire there and carrying embers to the bedrooms. At midnight the footman was up checking doors were bolted, servants abed and ensuring the security of the household. Consequently there was never a moment when Suzannah was alone. She attended breakfast, lunch and tea with the family, turned the music when Maria played the spinette and took her exercise in the meadows and orchard in the afternoons so her contact with Squire Martyn was occasional and always under supervision. Nevertheless he took every opportunity to be within arm's reach when they were in the same room, admiring her embroidery, asking her to bring him a glass from the server or to retrieve a dropped snuff box and at every turn she could feel his eyes on her. As she was so much in company she feared little that he would act immodestly but she was prepared for any eventuality.

One afternoon when it was wet Maria was supervising Catherine in the long room and Suzannah had to go downstairs to do some tasks for Anne Friend. She was to help sort the household linen and be taught how to allocate bedding and check for tears and fraying. She well knew how to repair any fabrics having spent most of her young life doing just that. She was sat up at the table near daylight with a linen pillow case whose edges were all come apart and was stitching carefully when the door to the small parlour opened and there stood Squire Martyn.

"Why Suzannah, Miss Friend not with you?" he enquired. She stood up and curtseyed knocking her bobbin to the floor. He stooped and picked it up, giving him cause to get nearer to her.

"Here you are my dear, what tiny stitches! Your hands are very deft aren't they?" "Thankyou Sir, I can turn my hand to most chores if I am shown what to do," she smiled pertly up at him. "I expect you have learned a lot of things at home, living in a country farmhouse with three brothers; not much you haven't seen going on I dare say?" "Going on Sir? I'm not sure I've seen much going on at home." "Are your sisters married girl?" "Yes Sir, I am the last one and mother says she will be thankful when I am off her hands." "And do you have plans to marry, Suzannah?" "Oh yes Sir, subject to your releasing me I hope to have a husband one day." "And what will this husband be like, do you think?"

Suzannah was well aware of his tone changing. This was no polite chit chat but a manipulation to get her to say she was sexually aware. "Well I think he should be tall and fine looking, though not so handsome. Mother says that handsome men expect too much. And I would like to be well set up in a decent house." "Indeed, so what do think is fine looking, Suzannah?"

She knew at that point he was seeking flattery not honesty so she smiled coyly. "Oh Sir I think he should be dark with fashionable attire, a straight nose, dark eyes and not be too young. I think a young man could not know how to please a wife." She looked slyly out of the corner of her eye at him. "So you prefer the mature man, a man of wealth and status to some callow youth who professes romantic love but offers you little."

"I do Sir, I would be very grateful for a husband who would take care of me in every way." Squire Martyn was now within a few inches of her seated form and was about to reach out and touch her blonde curls when Anne Friend appeared at the door.

"I am sorry Sir. I did not know you were within." She curtseyed deeply and glared at Suzannah. "Suzannah have you not yet finished that slip. We haven't all day you know. I am waiting to put it on the list and put it away now."

Squire Martyn made his excuses and the women curtseyed again. "Just you watch what you are up to my lady!" said Miss Friend. "If the mistress catches you flaunting yourself at the master you will be out of here with a bad character in no time!"

"I am sure I don't know what you mean Miss Friend. If the master speaks to me I cannot refuse to reply. I was being polite and obedient." "Well in your station you are employed by the mistress and it is her will you have to accommodate not the master's whims and fancies and just you remember that."

Suzannah was left wondering what might have happened if Miss Friend had not appeared at the door at that moment. How would she have repelled the master? She may be at the call of Rebecca Martyn but the Squire had the last word and when it came to material rewards she could not see Rebecca finding the will to do so whereas the master seemed an easy prey for a few kind words and a little dalliance.

The autumn days grew shorter and there were fewer and fewer days they could go out for leisure. Each month

Suzannah was allowed to go to church and go home with her family and return at seven o'clock after supper and her family were all questions.

"Do you sit at table with the master Suzannah? Do you meet the visitors when they come in? Have you learned to ride side saddle? How is your music practice? Does Maria ask you questions about us?"

"No. Mother, tell them. You were there. I am a servant just as you were, I cannot socialise with visitors and the master." However she did flaunt her status a little telling the family how Miss Friend had allowed her to wear one of Maria's cast off gowns and some undergarments. She had been given hair pins and a net so she had quickly taught herself to wind and roll her hair in a grown up fashion. She had gazed at herself in a real mirror, a metal reflector that belonged to Maria, and pulled her corsets and stomacher as tight as possible forcing her bosom up as high as could be.

She did not have any low cut dresses but she could imagine how tempting she could look. She pinched her cheeks to make them rosy and bit her lips to make them red and rubbed chalk into her teeth. Maria wore no enhancements to her beauty, nor did Rebecca but Suzannah had seen guests with coloured cheeks and lips and even patches. She had heard of the eye washes and unguents that fashionable women used to enhance their assets.

One day the household was in disorder and she heard that a party from Bristow were coming to stay. This was a shipping master, Mr Fenwick, with whom Squire Martyn had business, his wife and daughter and a young man from the merchant trade. They arrived looking green from the long carriage journey and the horses were all sweated and coated with mud.

"Martyn, don't know how you can live out here in the wild," said the husband. "These roads are atrocious," exclaimed the wife, "such pot holes and mud we almost lost a wheel right up to the axle and the stupid coachman did not see it coming. By Yate we were lost in a fog and could not find a way across the heath and it was only nearing Gloster you could say there was anything approaching a thoroughfare." She glanced at the household as if to live in the countryside was a capital offence and the state of the roads the specific responsibility of the Martyn family.

Rebecca stepped forward to greet them. "I so agree with you. William would have me travelling these roads every month but I refuse on the grounds of my health and my life. I doubt if I should be alive today if I travelled that road as frequently as he does. Such rocking and jolting in the carriage. Can Bristow be worth the terrors?" The Squire glared at her.

"Bristow is the new London my dear. All the fashionable folk would choose to live there. If you went out more with fashionable society you would have seen that you are missing all the wonders of the new city." "Well I am sure you are well enough acquainted with them for both of us," she retorted.

Rebecca was safe in the company of others and the repression she had to endure whilst alone with her husband was now able to be vented. Suzannah picked up the tensions immediately. The guests were taken to their rooms to refresh themselves and Suzannah and Maria prepared to entertain them with music and singing in the big hall. Before dinner Maria played the spinette and Suzannah turned the pages taking time to appraise the new men in the room. The husband was plump and wore a long wig, much powdered. He too appeared to have rouged and powdered cheeks, much to Suzannah's amazement, but she managed not to stare or smirk at him, averting her eyes and thinking of the chores she had to do tomorrow. His wife was a shrewish, insipid woman, scrawny and pale, who took great pains to present herself as fashionably as possible. Their daughter looked similar but appeared cowed and silent and took little interest in the girls playing, looking about her in distaste at the old fashioned fittings of the house. However the young man brightened all their spirits. Not handsome yet fine looking, smooth chinned with pale blue eyes and light brown hair of his own. He was well versed in pleasing his companions, made lively conversation, admired everything and made himself useful to everyone. His name was Robert Timms and Suzannah was delighted to meet any man who was not a servant or over fifty.

She kept her eyes averted until their elders were engrossed in discussing the government then batted her eyelashes at him. He was not dismayed and soon had eyes only for Suzannah and not Maria.

"And do you play Miss?" he enquired. "No Sir, I am only just learning thanks to Squire Martyn's generosity," raising her voice so that everyone could hear. "And I should not ever be as proficient as Miss Martyn." "But would you like to be proficient?" "Indeed I should Sir, if only to gratify my master and mistress in the trouble they have taken in my education."

Rebecca looked perturbed at Suzannah's forwardness. "Education is the gift of the fortunate to the unfortunate and promotes God's work," she said sanctimoniously. "We do not expect servants to become proficient; they do not have the breeding for it. Play again Maria."

Robert Timms stood near to Suzannah while she turned the music pages. She wore her 'hand me down' gown in blue flannel with white muslin sleeves and high neck and thought how much more she would impress him decollete. Robert Timms praised Maria volubly on her playing in order to please his hosts and remarked how charming the children were. Suzannah thought he may well feel as awkward as herself, neither a host nor a couple and clearly not wealthy. Both of them straddled the class and fiscal barriers.

The other businessman, Mr Fenwick, traded in tobacco and sugar and looked very grumpy. It would take a few glasses of porter to warm him up Suzannah thought. He and Squire Martyn joked about the fortunes they were making.

"When my galley, the Bella Maria, returns from the West Indies it will be laden with sugar and spices worth a King's ransom. Then you shall visit us in Bristow I hope, Martyn, so we may celebrate your generosity and my good business sense".

Squire Martyn smiled. "As long as she gets to the West Indies without difficulty. The Bahama seas seem to be treacherous".

"No need to worry. I have sent her with enough good ballast to keep her keel deep on the journey out and if they live I shall profit there too!" They both guffawed in delight.

Suzannah did not know the ins and outs of seafaring over the Atlantic but meant to ask Benoit what they meant by ballast. She had heard of ships going about the world and never being seen again and wondered how the wives and children of the sailors could ever cope with the anguish.

At dinner Squire Martyn bade Suzannah leave the hall and invited Maria to dine with them. Suzannah curtseyed and went to Miss Friend for instruction. She had never been without Maria before and she supposed the Squire did not like Robert Timms looking at her. She was given some mending to do by candle light, a bowl of broth and hard bread for supper and had to wait until nine o'clock before Maria was released to her charge.

"So what did they talk about after I left?" she enquired of Maria. "Nothing that interested me. They spoke of people they knew, of shipping stories, ships gone missing, ships miraculously returned from the East, new cargos, all things I have no interest in. They spoke of ships that can now go to Cathay and bring back pots that are so fine you can see through them." "And did Timms speak with you?" Suzannah pulled at Maria's corset strings. "Why do you ask? Did you like him yourself? He is not handsome looking but quite pleasing to the eye," Maria teased. Suzannah tugged hard, "He's the only man under forty who has ever been here! Why would I not be interested?"

"Well of course he spoke with me. He sat next to me at dinner and we spoke of horses and about my pony. He said he had a fine riding horse called Pegasus in Bristow and they can ride out of town to a great promontory overlooking the gorge where the river runs through a great ravine. Benoit told us all about it once. The docks are beyond there and at times the ships are eight or nine days against the quays and lashed to great booms to protect them from the south westerly storms."

Suzannah tried to imagine such a life being the wife of a handsome young man who had such stories to tell.

She helped Maria brush her hair and plait it for the night and so excited was she that she pressed Maria for more and more stories until Maria begged to be allowed to go to sleep. Suzannah could not rest though and crept down the servants' stair to listen to the raucous laughter from the dining hall while Mrs Fenwick and Rebecca withdrew to the best parlour to make polite conversation until their men wanted them.

For the next week the gentlemen mostly rode out, hunting or attending sports, and other gaming venues. They usually returned the worse for drink although Suzannah noted from her bedroom window that Robert Timms took his duties more seriously, declining stronger drinks and keeping a wary eye out for his master's safety and integrity. The women mainly stayed indoors, discussing goodness what as Rebecca was not familiar with urban concerns of fashion and gossip and clearly Mrs Fenwick was. They were accompanied by Miss Friend and the children were largely banished to the day room and lessons which meant Suzannah had to amuse both girls and manage Daniel as well. Being obliged to spend more time with his sisters he was peevish and tried to lord it over them but Suzannah kept a firm grasp on the situation, having brothers of her own, and although he threatened her with censure from Squire Martyn when he told on her she did not think Martyn would pay much attention, now he was focussed on her staying. Before dinner Daniel was required to demonstrate his abilities in latin, maths and geography and a considerable amount of information about shipping routes, trade winds and cargo values, and had been well schooled by Benoit for the occasion.

One evening Suzannah was required to help polish the silver and was installed in the back parlour alone. Suddenly Squire Martyn appeared through the servants door, rosy cheeked with wine. "Why Suzannah is this how you are occupied while we enjoy company," he leered at her. Suzannah's hands were black with silver polish. "Yes master. I am sorry I am such a sight Sir."

"Why you have a black smudge on your cheek my dear. Let me wipe it away." Squire Martyn bent over her and used his hot thumb to rub her cheek clean. "And what a rosy cheek you have my dear, let me check whether I have removed all the stain."

He pulled her chin towards him with his fingers so his red face and sour breath were close to her face and suddenly kissed her cheek. Suzannah pulled quickly away, raising her blackened hands to her face. "Oh master you should not," she said feigning embarrassment.

"And why not, my pretty maid? Do I not pay your wage and clothe and feed you? Do I not give you an education worthy of a squire's daughter and all for what? A little toileting and comfort to my daughter. Surely Suzannah you owe me a great deal, do you not?"

"I am sure I do master, but I would know how best to gratify your generosity Sir." She was thinking quickly now, not to repel him but neither to let him have his way, at least yet.

"I am sure I would be most grateful should your generosity include a more womanly gown". "More grateful, eh? How grateful do you think you could be, do you think Suzannah?" She was now standing on the other side of her chair but he came around behind her and could feel his hot breath on her neck. "Oh Sir I am sure your generosity would be worthy of my deepest gratitude."

He bent and kissed the back of her neck and she felt his body pushing her from behind rhythmically. Suddenly she was a little frightened of his impertinence and tipped one of the silver platters on to the floor with a great crash. Squire Martyn pulled away as footsteps were heard in the passage and one of the maids came bustling in to see what the noise was. "I am sorry Sir, I thought Suzannah was working here alone." "Tis alright Mary, ask Branham to bring more Malmsey wine to the hall." As he left he winked at Suzannah, making her skin crawl.

That night she lay next to Maria plotting her rise to status in the household through taking advantage of Squire Martyn's lust. If he gave her a new gown what else should he get for her? Pearls perhaps, or a coral bracelet, or a fine lace shawl. Perhaps she could keep him hot for a good while without losing her virtue and she enjoyed the idea of curtseying to his sour faced wife too. She must now speak with her sister, Constance about the precautions women knew about and how to manage men's desires.

It was only another week before Squire Martyn was due to accompany the Fenwicks back to Bristow and sail for London for another month and at every opportunity he attempted to brush against her or steal a kiss on the few occasions she was alone.

One day he came upon her in the servant's passage and grabbed her wrist to kiss her. Another day he sent the girls off riding then tried to wrestle a kiss from Suzannah on the way back from the stables. She laughed and reminded him he had not kept his part of the bargain and where was her new gown? In the end he remarked to Miss Friend that Suzannah shamed the household by having only one good gown and ordered that something more in keeping with her maturity would suit. He instructed Miss Friend to make up a new gown in dark blue wool for Suzannah while he was away. Shortly before he left he informed his wife that she should pay more attention to the dress of the servants who were in sight now they were entertaining wealthy guests. As this only applied to Suzannah and Ann Friend they both benefitted that month by new gowns and petticoats and linen caps to be seen in outdoors.

As the Fenwicks left Robert Timms kissed Suzannah's hand when the others were out of the house and complimented her demeanour and its positive effect on Maria's appearance. Suzannah for the first time felt elated that she had acquired the good respect and attention from a man she admired. Squire Martyn took the opportunity to squeeze her flanks on leaving and wink lasciviously. "I shall look forward to seeing you in your new livery, Suzannah".

Chapter Five

Cornfield Terrace

FRANKIE BURNS WAS pacing up and down her mother's living room. She had barely got over finding the last body at the flats, now there were police everywhere again. It was like a nightmare. All the questions and having to go into Gloucester Police Station. That, and having to get methadone every day from the chemist, had finally tipped her over the edge. She wanted some respite from the pressure but that only came with heroin. Her mother was uninterested in her daughter's pain. "You made your bed-you lie in it girl" she said more than once a day. All her own bitterness and frustration from her own youth was now being vented on her daughter and she felt a sense of satisfaction that she was not the one suffering now.

Inevitably the police knocked on the door. A young woman PC, Penny Wortham, who had no idea who Frankie was, was treated to a screaming fit, tears and Frankie kicking the front door with ferocity. From behind her her mother casually called out "She saw the last one. The body. Driven her barmy." Eventually the officer got in and was able to calm Frankie down and suggested to her mother that she needed counselling for post traumatic shock. "It's up to her. I'm not stopping her," came the lugubrious reply. The PC was not surprised at the effect on a girl who had probably seen more traumatic events than she had. She persuaded her mother to make some tea, leaving the room.

"Frankie, I get the feeling there is more to this than you've said. You're really disturbed by this. As far as I know you didn't know either of the deceased very well. Is that true or not?" she tried. "Were they your dealers or your boyfriends?" Frankie held her head in her hands whilst shaking her head in denial. "There's something wrong. Something spooky going on," she snivelled, but looked more encouraged by being listened to. Her mother came back with mugs of tea and she barely noticed the change. Two women living together who hardly regarded each other.

Frankie began. "Jake was always going on with his stories. He said there were undead spirits and they'd get anyone who told. He said they'd died in the past but were still walking about at night. He said he had control over them and anyone who told about them would be caught by them and taken underground."

PC Worstham was stunned. Surely this girl was old enough not to listen to fairy stories. Why was she so worked up? How had this guy Jake got so much power over her? Her mother handed over a grubby mug with ninja turtles on.

"See what I mean? And I'm supposed to be sympathetic?" she snorted. "She's got it off her Dad, he was half witted. They're all inbred them Burns's. She's got a half- brother carted off to the loony bin last year…"

"Stop it" yelled the PC. "Can't you see you are making it worse." Frankie by now was shivering and shaking and staring fixedly at the floor. "That's just the drugs wearing off," her mother got up and lit a cigarette. "She'll be alright once she's got her methadone. Can you give her a lift down the village?" PC Worstham thought it was good opportunity to speak to Frankie away from her mother and radioed in to say she was driving Frankie down to the chemist. On the way she got her talking again. "So how often did you talk to this Jake bloke?" "Not much I just heard what other people said. He didn't talk much to girls. Ready to sell you drugs if you wanted but not heroin which is what I was on up till last month." She seemed to be relaxing already out of the influence of her mother. "It was different with boys, they were like a sort of club. They believed Jake had some sort secret power. They used to meet at the bunker. Jake told them he'd put a sort of thingy on them to make them die. He's the one that made Paul die."

PC Worstham thought quickly, "Do you mean a sort of spell? a curse?" "No it began with an H." "You mean a hex?" PC Wortham. "Are you saying that Jake pretended he had put a hex on Paul Manners, the first body, and that is what killed him?" "Yeah, that's the word. I don't even know what a hex is." PC Wortham could not believe that this was part of her job. "It's an African word, it's like a spell but it's just rubbish. You can't put spells on people and Jake did not kill Paul that way. OK?"

"He did. He told Billy Smith he'd done it before Paul died."

"Paul Manners died long before you found him. Someone broke into the flat at some point. That was probably

Jake. He saw the body, nicked some stuff and told everyone Paul was going to die because of the power he had. When you then found the body everyone believed him." "So what killed Jake then?" Frankie looked really terrified now. PC Wortham sighed, "Jake probably died the same way, maybe dodgy heroin or contaminated needles. You're lucky you're out of it now". Frankie looked quizzically at her. "Jake wasn't a junkie. He never did heroin. I told you, he didn't have any heroin in his flat or I'd be getting it there wouldn't I?"

PC Wortham thought for a minute. "Frankie, where is the bunker?"

She looked nervous now. "I don't know, did I say that? You put me under pressure. You're not supposed to do that. Don't tell anyone I told you that!" She leapt out of the car and disappeared into the chemist shop. PC Worstham was left wondering what Jake would describe as a bunker. A basement flat? A cellar in one of the houses? Whatever or wherever it was it frightened Frankie more than anything. Penny drove slowly round the corner, stopped and wrote down everything Frankie told her in her notebook.

Back at Little Meadows she continued her door to door enquiries in Cornfield Terrace. Two-storey maisonettes, lots of kids, squalor and hostility. She knew from the initial enquiries that most of the families on the estate were either known to police or had children known to police. She now asked each family what the bunker was. The adults looked blank but she sensed a ripple of knowledge run through the teenagers. One boy almost piped until a look that could freeze water from an older brother stifled him but she wrote down the younger boys name anyway. No one knew anything. They knew Jake-not very well. No he never came to their home, no they did not know where his girlfriend lived. Their children did not hang out with him. Suddenly Jake Freeman had no friends apparently.

DS Benson was at Stonefield interviewing Rose. She had a weary, closed demeanour he had seen so often in police stations trying to interview teenagers with their mothers. They did not co-operate, full stop. They were not rude or aggressive they just blanked off what they did know. She did not even look scared; level stare, she looked you in the eye and said she knew nothing. He wished he could place a bug in the flat; when he left that was when they would start talking and he would hear the low down on Jake's activities. But this was Britain. Everything had to be done by the book.

Outside he stopped to draw breath before going on to the next flat. Were the occupants scared the police would find out something else? They knew Jake was a pusher, half these people were users, surely they would not be worried about revealing they had bought drugs off Jake. So what? Could be a paedophile ring. Maybe Jake started it off by grooming kids and the parents were making money now. But who were the customers? He had hardly seen any blokes around except penniless teenagers. These were women and children with no vested interest in covering up child abuse. Maybe it was photography? You got well paid for dirty photos. Judging by the state of their homes they did not have any money, so it would have to be drugs. He began to form a hypothesis. Jake Freeman had appeared on the estate two years ago, chats up the locals and gets them hooked on drugs. When they are he suggests they might like to have some glamour pictures taken in exchange for drugs, more and more obscene as they get more desperate. Then he starts on the kids. He imagined the conversations; "Give us the gear. I'm sick. I've done the job, give us the gear". "You're no good any more. You look like shit. Maybe your daughter could stand in". Or son. Or baby. He shuddered at the thought. Could women sell their children for drugs? His experience told him yes.

He finished off the last of the block and met up with Mustoe and Worstham outside. He liked Penny Worstham, she was tough, but not unapproachable and she could share a joke in the canteen without taking it seriously, but when it came to the job she was 100%. That was why they had picked her for the job. Thorough, intuitive and good with people. She would get more out of these people than he or Mustoe would. They had a brief exchange of intelligence and Penny told them about the bunker. Mark began to explain his theory. It seemed as viable as anything else. Somewhere there was a room or a place that Jake used that was not his flat. The teenagers knew about it and he used crazy stories to frighten them into silence. Their reward was drugs and access to a secret gang. They guessed that being such a small estate most of the kids here would know something about the bunker, probably the younger ones would give up the information more easily if you could get past their mother.

They decided to stop for lunch, let Penny and Mark finish the flats and formulate a plan to incorporate some unofficial intelligence; school teachers, bus drivers, shop keepers who sold sweets, youth workers. Someone had probably overheard kids talking and not realised the significance or bothered about what the bunker was. Someone must have seen Jake's movements and where he went regularly.

The body had been taken to the mortuary in Gloucester. David Champion had three bodies in. A knifing of an old alcoholic, a woman who dropped dead on a bus and Jake Freeman. He withstood the pressure to do Jake first, preferring to undertake his work in strict order. The alcoholic had been stabbed in a squat, living along with three other men. They had the knife and suspected one of the men, who had form for violence, as being the perpetrator. All present had given completely different stories; he had tripped and fallen on his own knife, a stranger came in and knifed him, he had walked in from the street with a knife still in him. Champion's work could tell them the angle of the wound and how long he had been left before being reported. Was the perpetrator tall or short, right or left handed. There were defensive wounds. Champion could tell them a lot about how death had occurred, where the blood would have gone, if there had been a fight and how long he had taken to die. After two hours he concluded that that his victim had been sitting down, unlikely in the street, the perpetrator having used the knife from a standing position, downwards into the aorta from the front-a right handed thrust. There was an immediate rush of blood that stopped as soon as the heart stopped, almost immediately. Defensive wounds were evident showing the man was awake at the time of the attack but did not stand up. The victim had plenty of old wounds, a mark on the scalp looked like a cleaver. Probably a belligerent drunk who invited fights. Severe cirrhosis of the liver, he probably had little time to live and was in constant pain.

Champion finished dictating his report, cleaned up and went for a coffee in the rest room. He and his assistant sat among evidence bags, cameras and the smell of death but had long been used to it. None of them were looking forward to doing Jake Freeman. He had come in at 10.30 am as they had started work and their initial concern was to wash off and keep some of the maggots, which could show how long he had been lying there. But not until they had collected every piece of potential evidence. DNA, body fluids, fibres, hairs; all had to be collected while they hung over the putrid body. It was a three person job and as they did not want to be there all night they decided to leave the dead woman until the next day. They could find no next of kin so there was less pressure while the police sought someone who could confirm her identity. They finished the chocolate biscuits, pulled up their masks, went to glove up and pulled Jake out of the cabinet.

Back in Stonefield the excitement had died down. Neighbours began gossiping in groups in their own flats, the cars and crowds of police having gone, leaving just uniform at the flat entrance. Penny and Mark continued along Daisy Bank and Little Meadows all afternoon. They met Marj McCormack and Evie Smith. The children had been sent off to school but it helped to get an overview of the relationships between adults and whose children played with whom. They had agreed to make a graph of all the children in the flats and maisonettes to see how many fell into the 12 to 15 age group that Jake favoured.

The elderly in Meadow Drive were far more forthcoming. Forced into proximity to Worsley's most dubious residents they spent most of the day watching the comings and goings of the younger residents. Penny found they were more garrulous in two or threes, trying to out-do each other in how much they knew. They could tell her which mothers hit and swore at their children. Who sent the children to school half-dressed or dirty, who came back drunk at night, who drove illegally, who regularly got the bus to and from Gloucester. They were ideally situated in Meadows Drive that led to the estate and was opposite the bus stop so everyone had to walk past the length of the terraced bungalows to get anywhere. All except the kids and teenagers who had nowhere to go.

The estate was surrounded by arable land with wire fences round, long knocked down to allow ingress. Around the derelict playground inroads had been made into a field of barley and there were clear paths across a rough meadow that led up to the old aerodrome. Other than that there were few routes to take. There were footpaths along the sides of fields where people walked their dogs or just let them loose but few people on the estate relished walking for pleasure so apart from occasional ramblers' groups the paths were overgrown.

Penny had her umpteenth cup of tea in Ellen Dowdeswell's pristine sitting room. Her neighbours, Margaret and Carol, had been looking forward to this all day. Ellen or Nell as she was known, led the tirade about the lack of police here when they were needed. "Vandalism, joyriding, fights. No one ever comes then," she steamed. "Someone had to die first. It's like a frontier town in the wild west." Penny commiserated and looked sympathetic but bit by bit got them to remember when they had seen Jake and his regular habits and journeys into town. It appeared he used to go into town in the afternoons two or three times a week by bus but also had a girlfriend who drove a car. Penny made a note of her description and the car which was a blue saloon, possibly a ford escort, tidy but old. This woman could probably tell more about Jake's lifestyle than anyone if she would talk.

At the mortuary David Champion had switched on his microphone and his assistants were opening plastic evidence bags and preparing labels. They reverted to special masks at once as the smell was horrendous and it was hard not to stare at the maggots, now still with the cold. They went over the clothes with magnifying glasses, David with tweezers, teasing out fibres and hairs that looked different from Jake's own and working their way down his shirt and jeans. Then they started to remove his clothing. Boots, socks, bagged and labelled. They cut away his shirt and trousers. The grey-green colour came first but as they hauled off the jeans, revealing his crotch all three stopped in amazement. Large black swellings protruded from his groin like tree fungus. The photographer was reeling but had to keep taking shots, this was a new one for him. "Christ what do these junkies do to themselves?" asked Anna, the assistant, "he's got veins elsewhere why use the groin? I'll never understand what they get up to." David cut away the underpants to save disturbing the abscesses and looked closer. He looked at the arms and feet. There was no sign of injecting anywhere on his body. "I've never seen this before even on IV users. I think we should prepare for notification."

Special procedures had to be undertaken for contagious diseases-the first, notably to put a notice on the door and telephone the authorities. David then called the specialist in contagious diseases and described to him what they had found. Normal septicaemia would cause blackening of the skin, rashes and bruising but not abscesses like these. These looked like they had swollen from within not from an external infection.

The three of them waited away from the body for the specialists to check their results. They looked anxious and pale. Only a few diseases were contaminatory after death and mostly from equatorial places. Surely Jake had no African connections? It was well to get an opinion before they started touching the body. Finally the telephone rang and David spoke for some time to the informant giving more details. At that moment the bell rang, indicating the police arrival. Mustoe stood outside the mortuary, a packet of strong mints in his pocket. Putting two in his mouth and dabbing his nose with Olbas oil. He did not mind being seen to take precautions but he felt it gave him a disadvantage with the pathologists to be seen as too squeamish. Of all the officers in Gloucester he was the one least affected by blood and guts. Mangled limbs, rotting corpses, pools of blood, dissected organs. He was as good as the doctors in dealing with sights and smells. Few pathologists had been able to shock or sicken him over the last twenty years. So he was surprised to be told on the intercom that he could not come in. He was formally notified there was a possible contagious disease within and the autopsy was suspended. Eventually Anna, masked and gowned, came to the door. "Inspector, your man may well have been a drug user and could have overdosed but it is likely what killed him was bubonic plague!"

Chapter Six

Rebecca

4th September 1687
Mrs Sarah Gurney 4, Cornwall Terrace Bath.

Dearest Sister,

Please be assured of my greatest love and affection for you and how I so miss your companionship and goodness in my ordeal. I do not know how much I can bear of my husband's cruelty towards me. This last three weeks he brought home the Fenwicks with that shrewish Caroline, his wife. Before she had stepped over the threshold she was full of criticism of our home, our practices and our staff. It was well you advised me in responding in kind for I had practiced in my mind several scalding retorts to put her in her place. She is so scrawny and sallow I cannot think how Fenwick can show her in public. At least William takes little notice of her.

I wish I could say the same for our new servant, Suzannah. From the very first I guessed it would be trouble to invite into the household such a forward and showy trollop, with her blond curls and blue eyes, she looks like an angel but she is that coquettish I know she is encouraging William in all his lewd ways. A week ago I came from the parlour and he was against her in the passage way leering and grinning at her as if something had occurred between them and all she does is flutter those long lashes and look up at him as if butter would not melt in her mouth. Now he has demanded that all staff be turned out in new stuffs so I have had to purchase velvet for the little madam as well as turn out Ann in a new gown. Not that Ann does not deserve such, she is such succour to me in my misery.

Every day he has been going out gaming and hunting with Fenwick and they return and drink themselves stupid. Fortunately Cowle has often had to get him up and put him to bed most nights although on occasions I have had to endure his attentions to my person. The indignities I have had to suffer in public are truly wicked and I do not know how I have displeased God in having to support this interminable degradation. Surely our upbringing and demeanour as girls was as moral and devout as possible. Never have I strayed from my duties as a wife and upheld the worth and dignity of our parents.

The Fenwicks leave in three days and William with them and it cannot be too soon. He tells me they are sailing from Bristow to London and he will return by horse but with luck in winter the temptations of the London stews and gaming dens will delay him all season. The last time he went to London was after Daniel was born and he was away four months and I was in such a sorry state that I was confined for much of that time with melancholy from the birth. You helped me so much in my hour of need then dear sister I cannot thank you enough. But I pray you please come to me soon. I know your husband has need of you at home but surely it is eighteen months since you came to me last and there will be no need to meet with William at all. I am sure he will not miss seeing you.

Not all is devastation. Although Suzannah is a little vixen I cannot fault her care of Maria. She has been so much more confident since we acquired a servant. She rides better, is more disposed to go out in the air and take exercise and is so much more diligent in her studies. Her playing is coming on so and I believe Suzannah will be able to play a little that they may duet. I have a mind to order some Italian music from London to stretch her mind and abilities. Perhaps if you came to visit soon you shall be witness to her prowess.

Catherine too is more devoted to her studies but I fear she does not have the wit of her brother and sister but may manage some accomplishments in time. She is such a sweet tempered child though and fortunately her father ignores her above the others so she is not spoiled. I just pray the example he sets of gluttony and lecherousness and incontinence is not evident in his girls.

My darling Daniel, of course, progresses faster than ever. He is proficient in riding, fencing and plays the lute a little. His tutor, Benoit, has taught him French and Italian which will serve him well when he inherits his father's fortunes and businesses, (God let it be soon). He does not like his studies and although I agree with Benoit that he should be thrashed for disobedience I pray to God it is not often. If Benoit were more gentle and encouraging in his ways my poor little Daniel should not have such chastisement.

I can see the vile habits of his father already intruding on his person. Only a se'night since he was witness to William's drunken behavior when he almost fell in the fire then lost his temper and kicked the hound. Daniel proceeded to kick the hounds at will before I threatened him with Benoit's cane. Whatever he sees his father do he will follow. He has been fed full-bodied wine and rich meats and on each occasion has been ill from it but will William heed my fears? No. It is fashionable for an eight year old to partake of French habits. Lord he will be sleeping with harlots ere long.

Sister dear, please have mercy upon me and take advantage of William's absence to visit me here. I cannot face the journey myself and Daniel would be such a charge away from his tutor. You may bring the children with you now we have Ann Friend and Suzannah as extra service to them. I search daily for your kind attentions,

your devoted sister,
Rebecca.

29ᵗʰ September 1687
Mrs R. Martyn, Worsley Hall, Gloster.

My Dearest Rebecca,

I am so sad to hear of the burden you have to bear. Our father was most remiss in favouring William when we were betrothed as I was better placed than yourself with my dearest Charles. At least you now will have the benefit of your children without the humiliation of William's unforgivable behavior. I hope you will be able to gain enjoyment from

them before the winter sets in properly. I do feel so grateful
to Charles for moving us to the centre of Bath when winter
is coming. The paved ways and raised walkways for people to
walk along are of great value in getting about the town when
the thoroughfares are beyond impassable due to the mud.
Last January the main road to London was so destroyed by
carriages sinking down and the volume of horses and cargo
travelling along that they have spent the summer reinforcing
the ways with clinker and stone out of the city at least to
Bathampton. The road south of the city is already paved in
stone as far as Walcot. They say that if we pay more taxes
every town could accommodate such byways. Your husband
is very sensible to go to London by sea and I doubt he will
easily return before April.

The more we delve into trade and commerce the more
the expenses of maintaining it. The boats in Bristow are so
many that they fight to secure a berth and offload cargo
and the expense is prohibitive. Charles has been importing
barley from Ireland, the price is so good, but last week a
barque carrying half his fortune was anchored outside the
harbour two days before there was access to the quays. I dare
say it is still cheaper and easier than London or Portsmouth.
Dartmouth shipped in at Liverpool last month and said
that he hardly had any profit once he had paid the taxes
and fees and wages. I am glad our business is set on dry
land where we can see it for ourselves. Barley is fetching
the highest prices now and all our wheat was taken by
September. Charles has been trying to get out of linseed
this year but it too has increased in price and we are awash
with the seedstuff.

Richard has done so well at his schooling this year and Charles is paying for him to enter Pagets in the town this term. His mathematics is ahead of his other subjects and I feel he will follow his father into trade no doubt about it. I only wish his writing was as good, he will never be able to woo the ladies with poems I fear. We spend so much time protecting the children from contact with other children in fear of the plague that I dare not feel comfortable about his attending school now. There was an outbreak of the cursed disease around the river where the houses are so cramped and damp and putrid. Doctor Spencer assures me that it is the malodorous smells from the accumulated excrement there down by the creek that causes the infection. He says that any household of scrupulous cleanliness and God fearing behavior cannot be infected. But I still do not propose allowing Richard going about the town mixing with his inferiors.

Last Saturday we were imposed upon by Alderman Oak and his large wife for dinner and I did wonder if he by his responsibilities would be associating with the underclasses and bringing their contamination into the town. He said they have burned all those houses now and no more contamination has been reported. I pray to God daily that our family shall not succumb to this demon. I do keep a fair amount of herbs about the house to ward off the vapours and see that John uses lavender in all the slops needed to wash the floors and doorways and we never open the windows on to the street in summer. Such an inconvenience. Just think how little you have to concern yourself with these horrors dear sister, deep in the fresh pure country air. God bless your little ones and keep them safe.

Now sister I feel so much more relieved that you will be by now without your tormentor that you can be at rest and gain some pleasure from your home and family. I have written to Phillip in Bristow and asked whether he would see his way to come to you with Rosalind, although I can never tell if she is with child again. As I last wrote in July she seems to have lost the last child she was with in May. Poor Phillip, he will never find another wife like his dear little Margaret. Never mind, Rosalind is a very sweet girl and he should not be alone with his children and Caroline is so in need of motherly guidance now. It is a pity Rosalind is barely older than her.

I am sorry I am not able to concede to your wishes and travel to be with you in Worsley but I am all the better to know that you have some respite. Please do destroy this missive as I would be mortified if it should fall into any other hands.

May God Bless you and keep you and your children,

Your loving sister Sarah.

To Sarah Gurney, 4 Cornwall Terrace, Bath.
12th October 1687

Dearest Sarah,

Be assured that your letters are consigned to the flame once I have received their sentiments and absorbed their feeling. It means so much to me to be able to express my true thoughts to someone I can trust utterly. Phillip would be balm to my agitation but I could not disclose my most intimate thoughts to him as I do to you. The physical humiliation I am exposed to by my husband's desires is known to you alone.

As you wisely said, now he is out of the house I can breathe again and feel the sun and rain and my children's love. What relief I feel. If only I could be assured of this release for a definite period. It is now autumn and then dark nights and wind close about the manor after dinner so that no diversion is available yet we are happy to reside under this roof while we women are autonomous.

This afternoon I accompanied Maria and Catherine in a walk to Netty Tump with Ann Friend and Suzannah. It was the first walk I have taken outside our manor this year and although rain threatened and a brisk breeze tugged at our caps I truly felt the good Lord will provide for my needs.

I beg you again to come and take advantage of this respite and share my joy. It is but a day's drive from Bath and we shall make every comfort for you here. Richard will enjoy playing with his cousins in the fresh fields and riding and fencing with Benoit I am sure and I cannot wait to see your new baby. You would feel so much safer here away from the fear of plague for a few weeks.

Thomas has slaughtered the pigs and we have such copious amounts of spice I am afeared we will be beset by robbers if we are discovered. Neighbour Shackley will shoot all our pheasants this year while William is away and we will have any game you will wish for as the park at Worsley always offers that supply. William supplies them with good exchange. If you come I will invite Mayor Pendy and his wife from Gloster as I am sure they do not come usually because of William's drunkenness and will only come in company. You liked his wife Eliza so much when you came the year before last. Little Catherine sends to you a note which I enclose. I do believe she is beginning to write a good hand.

Please honour us with your company as soon as possible, With much affection

Your dear sister Rebecca.

To Rebecca Martyn, Worsley Hall, Gloster.
12th November 1687

My Dearest Sister,

I was troubled to hear that your spouse causes you such shame with your company in Worsley. I am only glad that at the time of receiving your letter he will be out of your company for some time to come. I am sure that the Good Lord does not mean you to suffer for there is nothing reprehensible in your behaviour that could warrant such punishment. But these things are sent to test us and no doubt the Good Lord has his purpose of which we are not yet aware. Do enjoy what you do have; your beautiful children, fine home and more importantly your good health.

You cannot imagine how we live here in Bath forever in fear of one contamination after another coming from the travellers that are now so numerous. I am told in Bristow they fear the plague brought by sea so much that any ship arriving has to be set aside for three days to ensure no one can land with disease. The governors of Bristow insist that the port physician board every boat to ensure no sickness is there. First yellow fever from Africa, then black water fever from India, then plague from China. The rumours never stop from one day to another. If they are found to carry sickness they are caulked up like prisoners with his Majesty's Customs Men stationed outside. On one ship from the Arabian Gulf half the crew had died before docking and been thrown overboard. The other half died in dock and the poor families had to come and collect their bodies doused in lime and then pay for their caskets. What with the blackamoors dying in hundreds at sea or our crews infected by their heathen poxes I cannot see how we can benefit from these practices. Take them all to London I say where the pox rages regardless of all the docking.

I am surprised your William takes the risk of going to Bristow so frequently. In regard to that person we do not name I have heard that she is set up in Carters Buildings with her child and has been seen in her own carriage about the town. If any should be subject to the infections it should be such as her. My correspondent tells me she is twenty six and of merchant stock but came to Bristow as a child when her family all died leaving her an orphan. The Lord only knows where she has been these years between to get herself so well set up in the town but now has her suitor to pay her bills. I do feel such sympathy for you my dearest sister and think you well advised not to come to Bristow for all those reasons.

Happily I am able and most willing to meet your recent beseeching to visit you in Gloster. My Charles has completed the grain sales for this year and is due to go off on his rounds of suppliers before the winter closes the roads. He had not wished to leave me here to the mercy of the plague nor could

I travel without him now that Thomas is weaned, although I have left Richard with Darville enough times when we have been on excursions. We have agreed the coach for next month, the first week, and plan to leave here after breakfast to arrive before dinner with you. So hang up some hart ready for our arrival. I so look forward to Pate's braised partridges when I come to you. And I shall bring with me a case of preserved fruits we have supplied from Italy in glass; such a luxury we can get wholesale through Charles' acquaintance. And I shall bring two cones of sugar for your cook even if Fenwick has supplied you himself as we are awash with it here and Charles does not have a sweet tooth.

I do hope this letter finds you in better spirits than your last

Your loving sister Sarah

To Rebecca Martyn, Worsley Hall, Gloster.
19ᵗʰ December 1687

My dear Rebecca,

How delightful it was to stay with you all for so lengthy a time. I cannot conceive of the sense of restful restoration I feel now I am back in this great bustling city. The memories I shall carry are of warm fires, good food and fresh air and quietitude. I had forgotten what it was like to live with no-one outside the windows day and night. But most of all I shall cherish the memories of your good company. Never have I seen you so blooming and cheered. And the children so bonnie and charming. Maria is as true a beauty as was ever seen and her playing and singing are unsurpassed. Catherine so delightful a child and so amenable. Little Daniel, quite the little gentleman. I do not think you should fear for their father's turpitude when they have such a fine example of gentility as yourself. I thank you again for the perfect marionettes you found for Richard and embroidered crib cover for Thomas. It will be in our family these many years.

I was so pleased for you to hear that William cannot return to Worsley until after Christmas. For ill health he says! But a blessing for you. True it is not always best to be a household of women without a man about the premises but at least you can all indulge yourselves in a merry and innocent holiday together.

Will you keep the girl Suzannah with you for the season? To be sure she is a little wench full of her own airs and graces but I do think she genuinely cares for Maria and will not put her safety and welfare at risk. I did enjoy the little duet they performed together for our last night. Like two little larks they were. I wish for you most heartily a peaceful Christmastide and God's blessings on you all.

Your loving sister,
Sarah

To Sarah Gurney 4, Cornwall Terrace, Bath.
February 16th 1688

My dear sister,

The respite has come to an end. I received a letter from William yesterday informing me that he was then due to leave London by carriage. He tells me that the ill health that afflicted him before Christmas has now abated but left him with a raw chest and he cannot ride without making himself more ill. I just hope this few months of incapacity will have sobered him enough to reconsider the course his life has taken and to give more consideration to his family. According to the schedule he is in Oxford by now and shall be with us tomorrow.

So I shall need all my courage to continue but I shall consider my children's needs first. It is not fair on them to see me so despairing after they have witnessed my gaiety over the season.

I was pleased to hear of Phillip coming to stay with you in May before the city becomes too malodorous no doubt and Caroline must be so grown now she is ready to be introduced into society. If Richard is now to go to Oxford does he plan a career outside the grain trade? I do wish Phillip and Rosalind would come on here after Bath. I shall write to him again and beseech his support while William is at home. Phillip has such an easy way with him he may be able to deflect William's grosser habits.

Catherine has grown so since you left in December I have had to order worsted for winter clothes when we are nearly in spring. The girls are set to have new damask for the summer and William did write that he has several bolts of silk and tabby from the east in his luggage. Whatever he brings it will not be a welcome here. Daniel has really settled these few months out of William's influence and I do think he and Benoit are seeing from the same perspective now. He is so much nicer to manage now and more caring towards his sisters and I have noted on more than one occasion a returning affection for myself rather than contempt cultivated by his father. Oh that his influence could be curtailed for good.

Despite my distaste for the girl Suzannah I am thinking she may be of use to me yet. If he fancies her like it may well divert him from me and if she falls with child it is shame on her and her family not my household. I will discard her with a bad reputation and that will be the end of it. William can pay her off cheaply enough. It is sad but Hannah Garrod will cope no doubt. She has two daughters well married and all her sons in good trades. No doubt they will take her in again. As long as my Maria is not contaminated by this immorality. But we must live in hope Sarah and if William is worse for drink and gaming perhaps I will be writing to arrange a stay with you in March?

I wish you all my devoted love and miss you terribly

Your sister,
Rebecca.

To Rebecca Martyn, Worsley Hall.
1st March 1688

My Dear Rebecca,

How refreshed I was to hear your views on coping with your difficulties. You sound like a different woman since our sojourn together and I hope you are regaining your strengths and sensibilities that went on so long after the birth of Daniel. No doubt you have now got your measure of how things shall be until William goes away again. I am sorry to hear that your opinion of Suzannah is so low that you wish her degradation. She seemed a sensible, strong-minded girl to me, unlikely to either fall into immorality or seek to gain from her seduction of a married man. Nevertheless it is you who lives with her and can see the raw material.

Caroline was quite taken with the sound of her even with her funny country ways and she was pleased to pass on some cultured ideas from town to help Maria's education. I do not like this fad for colouring the face, it smacks of desperation, while these young girls should be enhancing their natural beauty. I should lock up Caroline should she appear with such reddened cheeks and lips as I see passing by in town. They tell me Bath is becoming the social centre of the West and Phillip should be cautious allowing Caroline to frequent such bawdy places. I shall say so when they come in May. The Seldons are coming to dine with us on Tuesday so I shall hear all the talk from Malmesbury no doubt. I shall write to you with any news and look forward to hear how you cope with the changes.

With devotion,
Your loving sister.

Mrs S Gurney, 4 Cornwall Terrace Bath.
30th March 1688

Dear Sister,

As you can imagine the return of my husband filled me with revulsion and I had to brace myself for his homecoming. To be fair he is a changed man since his illness and must have abstained from strong liquor for some weeks to behave so reasonably. He has lost much weight and is fitter for it. He has ridden out daily with Shackley and not become sodden with drink at least before dinner. I have born my duties more fittingly for a wife and I think William's hopes for another son have given him new vivacity. He often talks about the future of Daniel in business rather than coercing him into vulgar behavior. I told him Richard is now going to Oxford and I think he would like Daniel to follow suit. Lord, we have enough money to educate a dozen sons. William was undertaking business at Morley's Bank and there seems to be a fortune in gold which we can access with warrants from the bank in Gloster or Bristow against the bank's word.

William brought four bolts of silk from Italy and fine wool from the eastern marches. He has lambskin gloves for all of us and has even ordered Italian music for the girls. He bought for himself two books printed in Germany and maps for Daniel to learn from.

William told me that when taken ill with chest pains an associate called Robert Vaughan took him to his house in Ludgate and his servant and doctor ministered to him. He was sick all over the Christmas celebration and was in a high fever. The Vaughan's physician made him eat white onion broth and garlic and no worse has befallen their household. I do believe that his sight of God's Heaven has made him reconsider his ill behavior and invoked in him some remorse.

I pray you all fare as well in Bath and keep safe.

Your devoted sister, Rebecca.

Lizzy Lloyd

Mrs S Gurney, 4 Cornwall Terrace Bath
April 14th 1688

Dearest Sarah,

You will wonder at my delay in writing but beyond belief William suddenly announced that for Easter we would all be travelling to Bristow to stay with the Fenwicks. I cannot imagine what possessed him as he has many acquaintance there, no doubt who are aware of his shame in the guise of the madam of whom we do not speak, and to now parade me about as the wronged wife was intolerable. However I could not find any objection strong enough to deflect him as he was arrogant and oblivious to my feelings so we were bundled into the carriage and dragged into the mire of Bristow with all ceremony.

Fortunately the Fenwick's occupy a house in the countryside, so apart from using their carriage in the locality we only had to tolerate one trip into the town which as you can imagine was insufferable. We stayed two weeks and to be fair Mrs Fenwick was without stay in accommodating us in the most striking fashion. I was obliged to make pleasantries with her daily but more remarkable William was chivalry itself in company.

The girls were greatly improved by the varied company and I have to admit the society was a balm to my nerves as I am then less thrown into conflict with William. He was exceptionally generous too, buying all manner of gifts and presents for all, especially the children, and quite benign with all the visitors. If he were so behaved at home I may even make attempts at reconciliation.

We were also able to see Philp and Caroline with Rosalind on one expedition which delighted me and reminded me how charming a family I do have about the place. I hope I conducted myself adequately to make them proud of their sister.

I leave you with all good wishes for your health and happiness,

Your sister
Rebecca.

Mrs S. Gurney, 4 Cornwall Terrace, Bath.
28th April 1688

My Dear Sister,

I am sorry you have not had time to reply to my last letter and I hope all is well with you and safe in Bath. William has just this day returned from Bristow again and tells me that the Plague has extended beyond the docks and is now infecting the squalor along the waterfront into the town. I pray that there be no contamination in your area and beg you to come to us if there are any concerns of it spreading. William told me that in London it could infect one street but leave the rest untouched so God only knows what it is that infests certain houses. I worry that it punishes the immoral and that William's ways will bring it to us. There is strong belief among the ignorant that it is a curse from God foisted upon the immoral and slothful. At least you and I should be saved if that were so but I cannot say the same for William.

I am sure there is something going on with that girl Suzannah. I try in every way to keep her within my sight and Ann Friend knows to keep her in work every minute but she has her work to do and cannot be minding the child day and night. I have tried to ascertain from Maria if she knows of times when Suzannah is away from her side for any length of time but I cannot explain my purpose to her. I believe he has already tupped the little trollope. Last year William asked Ann to look out some old linen of Maria's but now I see she has lace on her petticoats and perfume about her person and why else should he provide for her in this way?

To Maria she is always available unless she is fetching and carrying or at the closet. How else should I protect her? During the winter there was less opportunity for riding or walking out, such wet and cold this spring has brought. There are lilies in the field beyond and the wood was full of windflower last month but we have hardly had a chance to see them. Benoit has arranged some exercise by suggesting games in the long room. The children have bats and balls and cups and play chasing games which does make them expend their strength but is very tedious to witness. Hopefully now it is nearly summer we will have more clement weather.

No weather will curtail William of course. I fear his drinking strong liquor is increasing again. Last week he came home from the baiting drunk and violent. Cowle managed to calm him down but I do fear for my safety when he is like that. Shackley spoke with me and says he is endeavouring to curtail William's fondness for the porter but he has many more friends to whom I do not have access who would lead him off the straight path. Do you have any news of Phillip and Rosalind? I did write to Phillip last month but without reply. Please let me know of any news good or bad and do remember you are all welcome to stay at will for as long as you wish.

Please write to me soon, your loving sister Rebecca.

To R. Martyn, Worsley Hall.
18th May 1688

Dear Sister,

Thankyou for your kind missive and my regrets for not replying sooner. Charles and I went to Somerset for him to complete some business and we stayed at Portishead with my husband's cousin Jeremiah, who is the priest there. It was a respite from the troubles in Bath and little Thomas is flourishing; he shall be two in summer and is already walking and scrambling over everything. Charles has regard for me to engage a maid for the children at last and Richard is still very obedient to Darville and so we get on very well.

I am amazed that William should so quickly force you to attend on Mrs Fenwick, almost strangers. Please tell me more of their situation and comestibles. If it improves his behaviours, however briefly it must be a good thing. And what of Philip and his family? How delightful it must have been to see them after these two years with so little contact.

I am sorry to hear that your situation has not continued to improve as hoped. I hope the fair weather and company of your children will divert your mind and that the demands put upon you can be banished often. I am sure I would not know how to cope as well as you have done these last years. God forbid but I wish ill on him for the misery he imposes on you day after day.

I believe Phillip and Rosalind are gone up to Oxford to see Richard's college there. He will be studying Classical History as well as Divinity so he will be too bright to return to our family. Please God Oxford does not succumb to this wretched disease and they are safe there. Phillip tells me Bristow has been struck in the lower town and precautions are taken everywhere and lime has been put about the streets and doors where there is infection and cloths soaked in lavender at the entrances to the houses. No one will touch water from the town pumps and carters have been selling sweet water from the hills and doing a great trade bringing in barrels from the springs.

I am now able to have more freedom to walk out as little Thomas' nurse is very reliable and he flourishes. I have discovered a new source of linen in the town which means I can examine it direct rather than depending on London tradesmen to bring it down. I am choosing several for myself and wondered if you would accept a parcel from us. I see the fashion is for lace and muslin cuffs. I have succumbed to the new fashion here as living in town it is very hard to resist the temptation and I have been at pains to order new wigs. Such a trial to be fitted and powdered and primped. I dare say you will chastise me for such vanity but it does seem so much less corrupt when everyone else does so.

I do think I may travel to Portishead again with Charles if he goes soon. June is such a busy month in the seed trade. If there is any news of travelling north I will write immediately and let you know if we may divert to your corner of God's earth.

With much affection,
Your devoted sister.

Mrs S. Gurney 4, Cornwall Terrace, Bath.

3rd June 1688

Dearest Sister

I greet you with good news. William has gone to Bristow again and it looks as if he may stay long enough for us to have some respite. Although it is abhorrent to think of that shrew in Carters Buildings claiming our wealth and good fortune, if it keeps William in Bristow this summer I cannot complain. For sure God is worn out with my prayers for relief and if this is his manner of meeting my prayers I am not one to complain.

Daniel not surprisingly waned as long as his father was corrupting him although of late William seemed more pre-occupied with his own affairs and was less likely to spoil the boy in front of guests and less inclined to press him to join in adult pastimes. I think Daniel felt it too as he has been truculent and sulky until William went away. Benoit is now more likely to use stratagems to get him to work as he is too old to be beaten with the rod. This is effective as Daniel is beginning to enjoy manly games and fencing rather than playing with his sisters and tormenting them. I hope this summer he will be able to ride out with Rawnslie's sons and begin associating with the better neighbours we have. If William is away these six weeks we will have a prospect of getting him good company and to learn society's manners.

As for me I will be less worried about my charge. So far she is not with child which relieves me. Surely if she were immoral it would have occurred. I met with Hannah Garrod in church last month and had to assure her of her daughter's good conduct but Lord I do not know how I looked as I am lying to her face if truth be known. I wish there was some way I could send the girl back home with some other reason for dismissal but I can think of no other maid as suited to Maria as Suzannah and Maria would be so distressed to lose her now.

It will not be long before I will need to see Maria in society and wedded but with William's habits frightening away half the county I fear she will be left a maid. Or worse she will be married for her dowry to some louch suitor with similar habits to William. I am minded to start associating with our mother's old cousins in Cirencester to be sure that someone of decent morals as well as fortune can be obtained to suit for her. We had hoped one of Lord Davenall's sons but I think they are already matched with the Wallesey girls.

Well I wish you and your family all blessed. I will be busy overseeing the harvest and preserving the fruits of our orchard. May you take pleasure in the fruits of your labours too.

Your loving sister Rebecca.

Chapter Seven

Jake's Demise

BILLY SMITH SAT in Marj McCormack's living room with three other youths and shared a gallon plastic container of rough cider. You could buy them for £2 at a farm over at Turley and one could get four people well smashed, enough for a good time. The boys were all part of Jake Freeman's followers, the inner sanctum, who had discovered the pleasures of cannabis, pornography and easy women at an early age. Of course you had to prove yourself, usually by stealing. Billy had burgled the back of the Ram in Worsley and got away with beers, crisps and cigarettes and no one found out it was him as he had no record. Eddy Cole had escaped arrest for stealing and joyriding cars by his death defying driving skills up windy single track lanes, leaving the police car in a ditch. Rob Vincent, who was older, had assaulted a police officer the first time he was stopped and searched and Nicky Rowe had a room full of stolen car radios and stereos by the age of fifteen. All of them were regulars at Marj McCormack's. They disdained the tiresome fumblings with girls their own age for full and abandoned intercourse with Marj on the grounds that once they had had few drinks you did not notice the ravaged face, died hair and flabby skin and body any more. When they were all together it was fun. They could egg each other on to do more and more outrageous things and pretend it was healthy sex.

Marj usually stayed in a dubious nylon dressing gown all day anyway. She was not too unhygienic, washed the sheets regularly, and she was not averse to mucking about in the bath either. Even the boys did not put up with smelly. All of them were shocked by Jake's sudden death and all of them had been in his flat after he died and before the police found out. Billy was the first. He had called round twice in the afternoon after the Bank Holiday and got no answer. He knew Jake should be in because they had decided to go into Gloucester at 3pm and meet a bloke with some dope to sell. Billy wanted to nick a new CD that was out and needed Jake as a diversion. The second time he knocked he had looked through the letter box and thought he could see Jake's boot sticking out behind a chair in the living room. Like the police he thought it was drugs. Initially he thought he would get in to help Jake if he had collapsed or something but having inserted a piece of plastic in the lock and shifted the door frame with a screwdriver and given it quite a good shove the door gave way. Billy stood and listened before going in in case a neighbour came to investigate. No one came.

Billy walked towards the living room looking at Jake's booted leg sticking out. He stopped at the door noticing how bad the room smelt. The curtains were always drawn but he instinctively knew that there had been little movement in the room for a few days. There were flies and a couple of bluebottles buzzing around too. He stepped into the room and with little experience knew straight away that Jake was dead. His reaction was to run but his mind was already throwing up possibilities. No one knew. Jake kept himself to himself. If he was dead he did not need his stuff now. If the police or doctor came it did not make any difference if he had no money on him or things were missing.

Billy was quick minded. Every time he had been in Jake's flat he had clocked something worth having. He had worked out a couple of places Jake kept his stash as well. After bracing himself to step past the body he went to the side of the fireplace where there was a loose tile, using his jumper sleeve as a glove he pulled it aside to reveal a plastic bag with some cannabis resin inside. Pleased with that Billy went into the bedroom. He pocketed Jake's watch, a digital alarm clock and some notes on the bedside table. He knew he must have some gold somewhere but could not guess where else to look. After a quick look in drawers and cupboards it crossed his mind to search the body. This gave Billy the shivers. Burglary was one thing but robbing corpses even affronted Billy's sensibilities. While he never believed Jake's stories about the dead coming back to life, being with a dead body was something else. Could Jake "see" even if he was dead?

Billy did not believe in God but he had an inherent belief that you get punished eventually by some greater power. Then his greed got the better of him and the justifications came thick and fast. No one would know; he would not get found out; Jake did not need it anymore; he had done Jake a lot of favours, Jake owed him. From the bedroom he could see Jake's face more clearly. The eyes were open and staring, there were flies on his mouth and nose, the dark bruises down his neck. Billy suddenly jumped out of his skin. Had Jake moved? He called softly, "Jake, it's me, Billy. Are you alright mate?" No reply. No flicker in the eyes, no movement. He had imagined it after all. He moved slowly forward placing his left foot and bringing the right up behind, his left arm outstretched like he was tightrope walking.

Sure enough Jake had that big gold chain around his neck; £300 or more, thought Billy. It took all his courage to put his hand on the clasp and pull it round to the front and undo it. The chain was smooth and big linked and moved easily out from behind Jake's neck. Billy stared at the face before he pocketed the gold. No sign of life, no breathing, good. He took another step forward and bent over the body pushing his first and second finger into Jake's trouser pocket. He felt a few coins and a five pound note in one. He had to push his arm under the body to reach his back pocket and the movement caused the stench to swirl around him, making him nauseous. But Jake's wallet was in there and plenty of notes in the flap inside. Not only that but two credit cards in other people's names. Billy thought hard. If he took them it was proof of a crime. They had probably been stopped by now anyway. Who knew how long Jake had been dead? No one would know how much money he would have on him. Billy took out the tens and twenties and put the fiver back in the wallet and pushed it back in Jake's pocket. "Thanks mate, sorry you're dead and that, but it's not my fault," he whispered.

As he bent down, pushing the wallet back in the pocket, he noticed Jake's right hand laying away from the body.

Jake's ring! He had shown it to them just the week before and said it was an antique ring worth hundreds of pounds. It looked old. It was big with an oval blue stone surrounded by pearls. He could not resist and plucked it off Jakes middle finger. He was so spooked now that he turned to leave, and as he did so he did not notice the putrid abscess where Jake' ring had been. Was that someone coming? Billy put the ring in his pocket and stood still listening. It was people in the corridor further away. Had he shut the door behind him? He waited what seemed like an age before stepping away from the body and crept out of the room. It was not until he had stepped to the front door and closed it behind him that he realised his heart was pumping and his legs shaking. Wanting to avoid the front entrance he walked to the fire escape round the back, and down the staircase to the garages at the rear. The route round the side came out at the fence and led to the track to the aerodrome and Billy felt he wanted to be alone with his spoils.

He felt good, he was a champion, a hero. He had got past that sleeping corpse and escaped alive. He kicked out at the nettles and brambles and dribbled a beer can up the path. In the drought the soil was baked and dry and the sun blazed out of a cloudless blue. Billy walked out on to the old runway and pretended to be a fighter plane taking off. Up and down he ran with his arms behind him in the familiar arrow shape he had seen when they were taking off for the Falklands War. He would be a hero one day like them.

After he had run and walked to the far end of the runway he looked at his spoils again. There was £230 in notes and about £50 in blow as well as the ring and the chain. He reckoned he had got about £1000 of gear in a few minutes and no one would know. He stopped. Not unless he told someone. He did not need to but what was the point if you could not brag about it? Who could he trust? Rob was the most reliable having a record himself and an entrenched hatred of the police. Nick had more to hide than most and would be least likely to grass him up. But wouldn't they all be jealous of him or resent him for not telling them first? They would want a cut of the cash for starters, a share of the dope and they would never let him get away with the chain, let alone the ring. Maybe he could concoct a story?

He sat on the concrete in the sunshine planning what to do with his money and what this meant for his present status. He needed to be able to show off his gains without being caught and that meant his best friends or strangers who would not question where he got stuff from. By the early evening he joined the group hanging round the bus stop "Hey guess what mate" he started "Jake's dead. Eddy gawped "What. How?" Nick looked shrewd "How do you know?" Billy already knew he had stepped over the mark by not informing them of what were public pickings. "Went round to see him this afty, doors open and he's on the mat- drugs I'd guess." He drew breath to gauge their reaction. "He looked terrible. All puffy and black bruises. Could've been beaten up but no sign of a struggle or nothing." Eddy stared. "You mean you went up to the body?" Billy half closed his eyes in arrogance "Yeah and went through his wallet," he bragged.

"You never put your dabs on everything!" Eddy scorned. "Course not. Covered me hands didn't I?" and demonstrated with the sleeves of his sweater. "And I got his stash. We can all go up the bunker and share it out. There's a fair bit."

Rob, aware that the youngster was queering his leadership, wanted to bring him down a peg or two. "I want to see Jake first." Nicky, aware of the opportunities at Jake's said "What about the other stuff, Jake's gold and that?" "Thats the funny thing," Billy said looking angelic, "I looked for his chain but couldn't find it. There's money with the stash though." He was hedging his bets. If they got something out of him they would be less likely to keep on about the chain. Rob cut through him. "I want to see for myself. Who's game? Nick was wary. "If Billy didn't find nothing what's the point? Someone might see us. Rob was suspicious. "Because Billy might be hiding stuff from us. Eddy was fearful they would have to look at a corpse and joined in. "Yeah we'd be seen and then we'd get blamed for the murder."

"So where's his chain then?" persisted Rob, remembering Jake always wore it. "Someone else must have got there first, who didn't know where his stash was. And he might have killed him. That chain's worth a load," said Rob to scare them. "I'll go myself tonight, before anything else goes missing." He looked at Billy. "You come with me. We'll meet Ed and Nick up at the bunker with the dope at nine o/clock. OK?"

Billy was unsure why he had to go back with Rob. Couldn't Rob go alone? He had, although he did not know Jake was dead then. It didn't get dark till ten o/clock on those sunny days so they sauntered through the playground teasing children, pretending they were going nowhere. They rolled some cigarettes behind the garages then slipped out of sight. Billy crept to the end of the garages; no one in sight; as long as nobody was watching out of their back windows. They made to saunter across the yard opposite to where

Jake's flat was, smoking as they went and casually talking about girls. Up the far staircase and along the landings. No one was about. Billy slid his plastic in the door and it opened even more easily. Rob looked impressed but this time Billy did not want to go in. The view of Jake's face and those open staring eyes was already haunting him. Rob strode in. He stood by the living room door and pushed Jake's foot with his own. Some flies buzzed in the air. Rob stepped back, the smell and the presence of his one-time friend lying dead overcame his need to be top dog.

"Christ Billy, he's a mess. Is that what scag does to you?" Billy was feeling queasy now and did not want to stay and look at Jake again. "Lets get out of here," he urged, but behind them they believed they had heard a rustling of people in the corridor. Both of them ducked behind the doors, holding their breath. "Rob, Billy it's us," Eddy and Nick stood in the doorway. "Shut it" hissed Rob "I told you we'd meet at nine in the bunker." "Well we wanted to see too," Nick challenged him. "Be my guest" said Rob, stepping aside from the doorway. Neither went near the door but looked from the hallway. "He's really bought it then," said Eddy. "No slaphead, he's just pretending" growled Rob. "Where'd he hide the stuff?"

All of them had visited Jake's at times and had seen him put things away. Billy pointed to the loose tile. Rob had another look and searched the fireplace and shelves for more hiding places. He warned them not to touch anything, leaving evidence about the place. "Billy's already been in. He can look. Nick thought Jake had a place in the bathroom. Billy edged the bath panel up. He needed the friction of his fingers to move it up so let go of his sweater cuffs. He was pleased he did. Behind it were shoe boxes with credit cards, driving licences, even a passport. More interestingly one with gold and jewellery in it. Billy quickly removed the stuff from the box trying to leave the dust intact and wiped the panel with a cloth where his finger prints had been. Nick and Eddy were looking round the bathroom door gaping in delight. "Ace Billy. We'll share it out tonight," said Nick, proud that he had known the hiding place. Rob had a look round the bedroom; there was nothing else to see. So they all left quietly and separately so as not to arouse suspicion. Billy turned to Rob. "Maybe we should leave the door open now so someone can see in? Someone has to see the body and tell the authorities. Maybe the postie?" Rob nodded his approval. It also crossed his mind the more people who went in to steal the more confusing any forensic evidence would become. None of them need deny being there, just not recently. That would explain any fingerprints, dropped hairs, shoe prints, everything. They disappeared into the darkness like shadows.

They met up at the bunker about twenty minutes later pulling the iron door aside and climbing down into the dark. They knew it so well the dark did not disturb them. There was a gas lamp Jake brought up and you could light it with a match. The walls were concrete and the floor mud. At the bottom of the back wall it had started to crumble in and Jake had fixed it with an old door and some struts to hold it up. They sat on beer crates and the car seat, lit the light and Billy opened the bag of hash. It was a big lump in clingfilm. Rob whistled, "Bulk buy eh?" He pulled out a lock knife and heated it in the gas flame then made a cut across the middle. "Who gets the biggest share?" They wanted to say Billy as he had had the courage to go in first but they knew Rob would be narked. "All equal then" he said and started dividing the block roughly in half and half again. He wrapped the two parts in clingfilm and gave two pieces to the others saying "Come on then roll ups ready".

Eddy and Nick brought out rizlas and cigarettes and made up the first two joints. They had also got four cans of special and they sat back and drank in contentment. "Here's to poor old Jake then," said Rob waving his can at the ceiling. "We'll have to vote in a new leader." Billy realised that without Jake there would be no dope and no more pornography, unless they got it elsewhere. There was a bloke sold it down the pub but at ridiculous prices. He was not prepared to pay that, anyway there were kids at school whose brothers could get stuff, they just needed to pay. Billy wasn't bothered. They could take dirty pictures of Marj for real. Maybe she knew some younger girls who would join in.

Actually he had seen a girl at school he was interested in. She looked real classy too, not a slag. Small pink mouth that looked like it had never been kissed. But she had a skirt right up to her bum and he could swear she had bent over to pick up some books in front of him on purpose. With his new found wealth he felt he could impress her. He had told the lads he got £130 not £230 so he had £100 all to himself, not to mention the chain. He would have to be careful when he sold that. Maybe a day trip to Birmingham? Billy had gone home before meeting his mates and put £100 and the chain and the ring in his room. His bed had wide steel tubes and the bed head came apart. You could put all sorts down there and his mother would never unscrew that, unless they moved and that was never going to happen. He was not bothered carrying drugs round here; there was no one to stop you. Gloucester was different, they had a drug squad there; pigs in plain clothes who scored and piped with the users then turned round and arrested them. "It shouldn't be allowed," he thought self-righteously. Pigs on puff and Charlie and they got paid to do it; and drive over the limit in car chases and drink drive. If you were the filth you could do anything and get away with it. Maybe it was not such a bad job, after all he did not have a record.

In Gloucester alarm bells were ringing. The mortuary was closed and all corpses diverted to Bristow. David Champion and his two assistants had to stay there all day awaiting a special decontamination unit. Champion had had to take samples of everything, put them in sealed containers and have them decontaminated before they were rushed to the special lab in Birmingham for rare and tropical diseases. Bubonic plague was spread by bodily fluids, pneumonic plague by vapour inhaled. It was highly unlikely any of them had inhaled the disease but the situation was so rare they had no way of knowing if Jake had had human fleas that could have bitten anyone. As the very suggestion had everyone itching and scratching they were none the wiser. By the end of the day they were all inoculated and tested and fumigated for fleas. A nurse in a plastic suit examined their hair and clothing for any sign of fleas and their skin for bite marks but it was generally felt unlikely they would get it and with preliminary hygiene would avoid passing it on. DI Mustoe got home at 10pm; he lived alone so had no one to notify. Mark Benson went back to his wife after informing her by 'phone. Champion had to tell his wife and three children another rare and exceptional facet of his job would impinge on them for a while to ensure they did not all go down with plague.

The big question was how did Jake Freeman get it? The other body, found two weeks ago, had not been tested. Old Dr Hargreaves knowing the peccadillos of his patient thought nothing of giving a certificate for septicaemia caused by injection and infection and the body had already been cremated. No one else seemed to have developed symptoms that he was in contact with. All GPs in Gloucester were alerted to look for unexpected cases of septicaemia. If Jake got it through fleas and went to Gloucester twice a week or more he could have infected anyone. On the bus; in a café; the pub or the cinema. Complete strangers living on the other side of the city.

Enquiries were raised about his girlfriend. No one knew her well enough to give an address. She was known in Worsley pubs simply as Annie, nothing more. In the interests of the community the news was not made public. Only medical staff, hospitals and ambulance drivers were informed. However it only took a resident of the Meadows to pick up the 'phone and sell the story to the Echo for a hundred pounds for Worsley to be virtually ostracized by the rest of the county.

Bus drivers eventually refused to do that run, people who did get on the No 17 bus were abused and no one else would travel on it after it got to Gloucester, except Worsley folk. After the first three days the bus company agreed to put on a special route that went there and back twice a day and dropped off a stop before the city centre.

The press were not reluctant to visit Worsley: "The Worsley Plague" read the front page of the Mirror, "Black

Death in the Cotswolds," read the second page of the Guardian, "Plague town cut off," Times, page five. The front page of the Sun had a vampire bat transposed over a picture of Worsley town centre. "Mystery illness bites," said the Echo. No one in Gloucestershire wanted it to be the Plague. Resonances of six hundred years previously when the Cotswold villages fell to dust, arable fields abandoned, farmyard stock let wander. Deep in folk memory the terror was struck again into Gloucestershire.

The Department of Health reminded people it had only one definite case, no one had reported any illness since the body was found and it was thought to be over a week now since he died. Health advisors set up a mobile education unit in Worsley to reassure and advise people how unlikely contamination was outside of Jake's home and housing staff were sent to enquire of every flat and bungalow to make sure no one was lying ill in their homes and rat catchers were despatched to all parts of Worsley to kill off every possible carrier from rats and squirrels to bat colonies and feral cats.

Chapter Eight
Suzannah's Dilemma

SUZANNAH WAS BEREFT when the Fenwicks and Mr Timms left Worsley Hall in October. She brushed her gold curls until they shone and put on her blue gown and pinched her cheeks before standing on the steps to wave goodbye. With the Fenwicks went Squire Martyn and Suzannah felt torn by the conflicting emotions. She wanted so much for Robert Timms to stay and Squire Martyn to leave, but where would it all end? What would the likes of Robert Timms want with a serving girl, however pretty. He needed a wife of substance who could enhance his career, but she was sure she could achieve that if she only had access to Bristow. There she could study the trade and behaviour of other wives and see what constituted a clever and supportive wife. On the farm being able to cook, clean and sew were most important; no woman was involved in the farm work in a city, where men went off to sea for months, the business would need to be overseen by the family to ensure they were not being cheated or ill advised. She would need to know about banks and so forth.

No one was going to take her to Bristow except Squire Martyn who was becoming increasingly feverish towards her. At every turn his eyes were upon her, every time she left the room he made excuses to follow and she became intoxicated with her power over such a man. Even talking to Timms she could see his jealous rage unsuppressed and she enjoyed the power she had to degrade him. Once they had all left for Bristow her world became a tame and listless place full of women's talk and boredom. She only looked forward to Christmas when she was promised she could return home overnight and spend Christmas Day with her parents. Constance and her family were also due to spend Christmas in the family home and they were all excited by the prospect.

In the meantime Mrs Martyn's family came to stay and Suzannah was greatly comforted by the ease and naturalness and sobriety of the Gurney family. Although she was charged with the entertainment of the little boy and occasionally the baby, they were endearing children and made her wistful for her own offspring. Sarah Gurney was so different from Rebecca, so cheerful, plump and kindly and her husband Charles a mellow and dutiful husband. Suzannah was almost ashamed at the tricks and schemes she had been plotting against the Martyns, so generous were the Gurney family.

The Gurneys were due to leave before Christmas and Squire Martyn expected to return but on 17th December Rebecca received a letter from London by courier, to say Squire Martyn had been laid low by a fever that affected his lungs and was unable to move from his bed. He had been taken in by a Robert Vaughan and his physician who assured Rebecca of their full attention to his needs and to keep her informed. The parchment and handwriting were of highest quality and it was clear Squire Martyn had friends of class and status as well as honour who would undertake to serve him as well if not better than at home. Suzannah wondered that Rebecca would not feel obliged to travel to care for him herself but the possibilities that he was with another woman or was suffering from the pox would have discouraged any liaison between them. Despite the possible censure she may receive Rebecca decided to remain in the country.

So, as Christmastide started they were all left alone at Worsley Hall, Benoit, Walsh and Cowle the only men available in the household. On Christmas Eve they walked to church with a thick frost on the ground and the candles in the church at midnight mass the only warmth in the building. Suzannah's teeth were chattering before they got to communion, despite her thick wool cloak and fur gloves and she was ecstatic with delight that she should be at home with her own dear family that night. Her mother and father, Constance, her red cheeked husband, Frederick; all were beaming at her across the aisle until she could fling herself into her father's arms as the bells rang out for Christmas Day.

"Suzannah, what colour, what grooming, your gown and cloak, you look so grand," exclaimed Constance.

"You look too fine to come back to our meagre home," laughed her father.

"Oh father, there is nowhere I should rather be than in the bosom of my own dear family." She made her farewells to the Martyn family and embraced Maria who would miss her the most and was genuinely sorry to say goodbye to her, if even for a day or two. She did not envy the solitary and cheerless Christmas with Rebecca and Miss Friend that the girls would experience. Perhaps Maria's mother would let her sleep with her tonight? Rebecca was pleased to let Suzannah stay two nights with her family, a plan Squire Martyn would never have tolerated wanting her at his beck and call at all times, so Suzannah was relieved to have her family to herself for three days.

On returning home Suzannah shed a tear or two for her own modest home. The brazier was kept going when they returned and they ate cakes and ale before they went up to bed. Her little room in the eaves, its tiny gable in the thatch, her earthenware washing bowl and the rag doll she cherished, all laid out on her bed. She had to share with her sister May as Constance's boy, Richard was put in May's bed, but it was Christmas and time to be a daughter again.

As Suzannah closed her eyes in her own bed, a hot stone wrapped in sacking at her feet, she wondered if the role of schemer, seductress and mistress would be hers in the following year. Maybe Squire Martyn would die first of the pox in London, but then how should she ever get to see the Fenwicks and Robert Timms again? She wished so fervently that Timms would write to her and send a sign or token of his interest but there had been nothing.

On Christmas Day she awoke early. May was jumping about wanting to go downstairs to see if she had the new hairbrush and petticoat she so wanted, ribbons, minced meat tarts, dried fruits from the levant and sugar sweetmeats. They got up together and washed and dressed in the freezing room as quickly as possible and met with Constance and her baby in the parlour. The children all waited excitedly for their father to let them open their presents before attending church again. There was a great flurry of activity in the house and Suzannah felt like her own childlike self again. Only a year ago she had been a green, naïve child and how much she had learned this year. Not only the spinette and French and mathematics and geography but manners, etiquette and social climbing, manipulation and coquetry, qualities her family despised.

There was no spinette to show her family her prowess but she sang at morning prayers with a little Italian madrigal for the family which touched their hearts. At church the curate and the smith's apprentice stared and stared and she knew she was now above their attention and would never now consider an attachment in the village. She tried not to look superior and adopted an expression of compassion and devotion and did not make eye contact with either.

Rebecca brought the children to church. She wore her mantilla under her cloak and the pearls and coral ring Martyn had given her. Without him the family looked relaxed and happy and Maria in a dark green gown and Catherine a lighter green both had red ribbons in their hair and looked a picture in their own pew at the front of the nave. Daniel wore a feather in his hat and pretended to be the man of the family. He took Catherine on his arm into church and neither smirked nor yawned for a whole hour. The bells rang out and Rebecca acknowledged Hannah's curtsey.

"I do hope our Suzannah has commended herself to you, Ma'am, and is obedient to your wishes?"

Rebecca was a little flustered. "She carries out all her duties to our satisfaction and is a credit to Maria. She has taken to the spinette and keeps her charges well attended and guides them diligently in their lessons and leisure" she responded.

"We are so grateful to you Ma'am. Should she give you any reason for complaint do not stay your hand and speak with myself or my husband". Suzannah winced as she thought how Rebecca would explain that their daughter was planning to use her power over Squire Martyn to acquire jewels and fine clothes.

They gave their greetings to friends and neighbours and returned to their respective homes. Suzannah sat down to her family's table of eight to herb bread, roast beef and pies and a suet pudding with raisins and honey. She received a new cap from Constance and Charles, some music from her father and a hand sewn linen nightdress and cap from her mother. She could not have been happier. After lunch she managed to seclude her sister in the bedroom and engaged her in conversation.

"Dear sister I do miss having a friend to confide in" pleaded Suzannah. "Pray tell me about the birth of little Henry; was it painful?"

"Yes it was but all was forgotten when he was put into my arms. I shall never forget the love that flowed out of me that day; more than I have ever felt for Charles."

"Did it hurt getting with child sister, for I am afeared of what marriage would bring?"

"Hush now. A woman's duty is to her husband. Choose one well and he will be kind in these matters. The begetting of children will be a pleasure not a duty."

"But does it not always result in childbirth Constance?"

"It is the will of God whether we are blessed with children, Suzannah why should you be afeared?"

"Because cousin Sarah died in childbirth and I would be frightened to give birth at a young age. Is there anyway to stop it?"

"Childbirth is a blessing from God. Why would you want to stop it?"

"I am only fifteen Constance and all these duties weigh heavy on me."

Constance was a woman of the world now and knew her sister well. She was not the girl to be anxious about natural interactions of people and suddenly she started to comprehend what Suzannah may be referring to.

"Sister, is this to do with Squire Martyn? Does he interfere with you? He is renowned for his lechery. Is this your fear?"

"Oh sister he is a fearful man. I keep my distance from him, such lecherous looks he gives me and has forced his person upon me in passages and when the servants are absent. I truly think he means to have his way with me."

"Suzannah you must leave! Tell father and get away now. Or is it too late?"

"Nothing has occurred yet. The master is sick in London for now, he may even die! I cannot leave. I have no duties at home and I cannot be kept forever. There are no suitors I would choose in the village. I was not as lucky as you sister."

"But if he returns and forces himself on you, and you are with child he will throw you out and your child will be given away and you sent to the workhouse or worse."

"How would I explain why I left? Rebecca would know and I would be an outcast on my own community. I have to manage this as best I can. My life there is more than I could ever expect from marriage and I do have a fondness for Maria."

"Well I did hear from that old hag who used to live over at low bottom that you can stop a child coming if you wish," she drew nearer to Suzannah's ear, "you have to soak a pad of cotton in vinegar and push it right up inside yourself and that will stop the baby coming. It was Mathilda Henshaw that heard it from her and she was that fertile she was with child every year and she paid a silver penny for the advice. But she did say it worked."

"Do you want to have more children Constance?"

"Indeed I do. It is what every good wife should strive for."

"But Squire Martyn's wife is afraid of her husband and does not want to beget more children by him."

"Not all husbands are as brutish and errant as Squire Martyn. She married him because of his wealth and her family had business with him in Bristow so the fortunes were combined. But his success has made him arrogant and his propensity for strong drink has debauched him. Gossip says he has a mistress in Bristow as well. He can well afford it. Maybe he has a mistress in London as well. It suits him to have a wife who chooses to stay at home and not go into society. I am sure he would want more sons though. How does she repel him?"

"They are at war at all times. They have separate bedrooms and I heard such a noise when she barred the door to him once. He smashed the lock off the door with the butler's shelalegh." Constance could not suppress a giggle.

"Then he still has his way with her. Maybe he will just enjoy the chase with you. Do not give in to him. He cannot force you, that is an offence and you could apply to the magistrate." Suzannah looked pensive. Constance embraced her. "Well stay close to Maria. He would not shame his own daughter. Do you sleep in her bed?"

"Yes I do but when she has lessons in the day I am wanted to do work in other parts of the house and I think he arranges for me to be alone so he can come upon me when the servants are ordered elsewhere and they cannot gainsay him." Constance hugged her, "I am so sorry he is a trouble to you. Is he in town for much longer so you can enjoy the company of the girls without this burden?"

"Yes and not only away but sickening with a chest complaint that means he cannot walk at all. I hope it is the plague!"

"Do not say that sister. What can he have done so wicked to warrant such a punishment?"

"I do not like him or the way he treats his wife, Constance. I do feel I am in danger if I refuse him. He will not mind a young servant girl."

"Just stay with the others at all times and if you are required to work go where the other servants are in hearing. I am sure Rebecca would not let him summon you else?"

"No that is true. How could she allow a harlot to share a bed with her daughter?"

The sisters hugged, the room so cold they could see their breath, so repaired downstairs to where the fire was hot and red with oak logs and the posset was warming in a cauldron above it. Suzannah realised for the first time in six months of being away from home how much she had changed. She had left home confident but ignorant about how she would control her situation. Now she felt so many pressures upon herself. The desire to please her parents and sisters and keep her post, the wish to make better acquaintance of Robert Timms and to be a credit to such a man, her growing loyalty to Maria and Catherine. All these contradicted her original goal to make the most of the family to her own advantage and walk away. Did she want to spend her youth as servant to Squire Martyn while Maria grew up and married and then spend another two or three years bringing up Catherine to be married. I would be twenty five before I would be thrown out back to my family or if I please the Martyn's sold off to someone I do not love and nothing to show for it, she thought. No, if I am to make anything of myself I must be mercenary and not displease Squire Martyn or his wife and somehow get to Bristow as a prize for any young businessman there.

CHAPTER NINE

THE AERODROME

JAKE HAD NOT had a particular local. He most often went in the Ram with Annie, never went in the Coach and Horses where Rose cleaned but, but dropped into the Queens Head and Black Horse often enough. He was not a big drinker either but the landlords could never catch him dealing drugs even if they thought that was what he was doing. He played a bit of pool, darts and liked chatting to the gangs of males who did little else in Worsley. A night out with the girlfriend was most likely dinner at the Little Chef on the A38. He had no apparent friends and even Ron Beeny made out they never met outside of the Ram and knew nothing about him. Police and press alike found Worsley a closed shop. Billy, Eddie and Rob were keeping a low profile. While they were prepared to put on a front for the police they needed not to be noticed or have anyone draw attention to them. They sauntered about at dusk warning the younger kids to keep their mouths shut and reminded them about the walking dead that Jake talked about, suggesting that now they were the keepers of the secret information and knowledge of these things. Threatening to unleash a zombie/ vampire on anyone who told stories about them was a good way of keeping the fuzz off their backs.

Marj McCormack had her own vested interest in keeping quiet as well. Despite her alcoholic state she was fully aware that with facts and dates she could be prosecuted for corrupting youngsters. She was happy to frolic with known participants like Billie and Rob but was fearful of kids like Danny finding out. That Rose was a queer one; too law abiding to be trusted.

Rose was trying to keep an eye on Danny. Asking casually of other Mums where their children went in the balmy warm evenings, smelling his clothes for cannabis and trying to persuade her sister to come up and take them away at the weekend. No chance with the threat of plague in the air. Her sister was blunt. "No chance Rose while that plague is about. No harm meant but I have my kids to think of."

Even her cleaning job was suspended for the week; that was £6 short she would be.

Evie Smith was perplexed about Billie. He was so moody these days. One minute friendly and chatty then furious because she had gone to clean his room. He was always out and when he came in went straight to his room. She noticed he was staggering once and she was too anxious to ask him if he had been smoking cannabis. She had no aversion to it and had had the odd puff herself but he was only fifteen. Having him around the house all day was painful too. He slept till noon, demanded food then went out in a flourish, slept some more and went off at seven to join his mates. At least he was not mixing with the likes of Jake any more. Rob and Eddie were a bit cheeky but they were nice lads underneath and she never liked the look of Jake. It was so much easier having girls she thought.

At the Meadows the press sat in cars twenty four hours a day outside the flats where Jake had died, alongside the health van and the rat-catcher by day. For the residents it was entertainment to interrupt their usually boring routine. The old folk tutted and tittle-tattled outside their bungalows and the children pestered the reporters for money offering to tell tales of sex and drugs for a fiver and the teenagers threw stones, spat and shouted abuse. The usual weekly visitors, Social Worker Helen Bourne and drugs workers Alice and Colin, who came to check out teenagers already know to the law and children on their "at risk" lists and to see young Mums with little incentive to give up drugs, crossed paths all day. None of them had seen any evidence of sickness elsewhere and were perplexed. Jake had had no truck with either service so was not known to anyone. They chatted with the health workers and rat catcher and kept each other informed. The police backed down; this was no murder and while Jake's possessions had been burgled there was no one to put in a complaint. DS Benson was left to wind up the enquiry and collect all the statements Penny and he and other constables had taken from door to door and pub to pub and shop to shop. None of the adults were any wiser about the site of "the bunker" either. None could think of anywhere in Worsley and the youths were not minded to tell. Requests were put out to check outlying farm buildings and sheds but no information came back.

On June 7th Helen Bourne was in her Fiesta, sweat pouring down her forehead on the first hot day of summer. She was leaving Little Meadows behind and God, what an awful day she had had so far. At three houses she had visited all the school age children were at home. It was four weeks to the end of term and there was little hope of persuading them to return now. No hope of taking exams, no hope at all really. She had called in at Frankie's on the advice of police and clearly the girl was in a state of neurosis as well as addiction. Helen had contacted Alice to get involved but she could not help feel there was something much deeper going on that Frankie was scared of. Her mother was indifferent not abusive and that left nothing much for Helen to do. She had introduced Alice and left them to talk.

Had her job always been this futile? As she drove the mile into Worsley the picture of an ice-cold lager came into her mind and she could not drive it out. She was not supposed to drink at work but who would notice? She parked in the car park of the Coach and Horses and unstuck her skirt from her rear as she climbed out of her hatchback. The golden liquid, ice-cold and condensing water on the outside of the glass never looked so good. Avoiding the sun and overcrowded bar she chose the darkest corner inside next to the inglenook and was surprised to find herself next to an elderly man, tall, moustachio'd and rather chatty.

"Feeling the heat?" he enquired, "I can't take it these days. Always stay indoors. I've come down for a few days to meet an old airforce chum. Are you local?"

Helen explained that she lived in the Forest, far away from Worsley.

"We were stationed here at the end of the Battle of Britain," he chattered on. "People always associate it with Kent and Sussex but we had our job to do as well. It wasn't half bad either, being in the Cotswolds in mid-summer. We were on Worsley aerodrome. Do you know it?" Helen said she knew there had been one once but had not actually seen it. She was not sure it still existed.

"Oh yes, it's there alright, the airstrip. Flew up there a few times in a tizzy. Never been so pleased to see an area of ground before or since after a raid. Half my mates died out there." He waved his hand vaguely to the south. "We were based up there but billeted in the town of course. Lots of pretty land girls here in those days. I married one!" he smiled wistfully. "We both came from London you see. She died last year; forty years married we were."

Helen smiled in compassion. Her world was so transient and unsure and so different from this man's experience. Her boyfriend of two years was already getting itchy feet and talking about travelling and she had only just started her career. This man had been happy to settle down for forty years with a girl he met in the war. Maybe wars focused your mind on what was important. He rambled on regardless.

"Oh yes, the girls used to plough up there, with horses mind you, right up to the airstrip. She was as pretty as a picture, golden curls, freckled face. When we took off I'd always look to see if she was watching. Last thing I thought of till I got back."

Helen stifled a yawn. The lager was going down a treat.

"Funny how we met. I was on standby when suddenly three gerries came out of nowhere shelling the airstrip. We had to run like hell and into the air-raid shelters, no time to scramble. Just as I got there I saw three land girls coming the other way. They'd left the horse and legged it. We all fell into the shelter and I fell over and she landed on top of me! In the dark! Didn't know it was her until I got up and lit a candle."

Helen downed the last of her pint and a car horn sounded from outside. "Oh that's my lift," said the old gentleman and got up nimbly for his years. Suddenly Helen was struck and ran to the old chap who was getting into a smart BMW. "Where did you say the shelters were?" she gasped. "Only the one my dear, back of the hangar, underground."

His car disappeared over the brow of the hill and Helen was left alone on the pavement. Air raid shelter? No one had mentioned that before. When she got back to her office she telephoned the police. "Penny Worsthorne? I think I may have found your bunker."

Penny was on to Mark immediately. He was starting another enquiry in Churchdown and was hoping there would be an end to the Worsley case. She was keen to examine this bunker if it was such a draw to youngsters. It could be a drug den or something far worse taking place. She felt it was the police's duty to know at least the possible sources of crime. Often they just got intelligence and left the premises alone knowing it was a likely hit when something was going off. It was better to have the knowledge rather than close somewhere down and then have no idea where kids were meeting.

"Mark, this could be the answer we are looking for. Maybe there is some sort of infection in there or someone still dead or dying. We have to check it out." Mark sighed. "I've got three burglaries to sort out and Mustoe has said no more resources to be spent on this case. Anyway, how did you find out about it?" "It was that social worker Helen. She got talking to some old bloke who had been stationed there in the war and told her there was an air raid shelter. Fits the bill, near the estate, buried underground and no one goes there.

She egged him on. "Come on Mark, it would only take an hour to go up there and root around. There's nothing else there. It's not as if we had to search a lot of buildings."

Mark was curious. He had been a member of a secret gang when he was ten or eleven and he could recall the excitement of having a den that no one else knew about where they could hide out. For him it had been an old shed in the woods, probably a woodman's hut or a gamekeeper but they had enjoyed making it special and putting their own stamp on it. Smuggling bits of old seats from his parents garage, a hurricane lamp and candles. He remembered the fun they had hiding away and the puzzlement of his parents wondering how he could be out with his friends all day, even when it was raining.

"Ok I'll spin some yarn to Mustoe. I'll bring a torch, you bring evidence bags and stuff. Have you got a jemmy and a hammer in case we have to break in the door?"

Penny wandered round the station to the equipment room where they kept the shields and helmets and persuaded the custodian to let her have a door ram, jemmy and heavy duty gloves and a large torch. She signed for them and bagged everything and put it in the boot of her car. She then waited for Mark to get back to the station before they set off towards Worsley.

"Can we get there by car?" she wondered. "I can only remember the path out of the Meadows." Mark looked at the map. "Yup. The road was the one through the estate but it was cut off when they built the flats. Looking at the map we'll have to park by the flats. Pity the watch has been taken off. We'll probably have half a car left if we leave it there." As they drove into Stonefield and rounded the flats the youths clocked them and stared. A police car was only trouble. They tried to make as little fuss as possible but taking the big bag out the boot and walking towards the field the whole estate would know what they were up to.

Rob Vincent was watching from the corner of Stonefield. He threw down his roll up and ran off to Eddie's flat. Eddie was still in bed although it was afternoon and he banged the door for some time before he got an answer. A disheveled Eddie opened the door dressed in baggy shorts and a dirty T shirt. "What the hell are you going on about," Eddie grumbled letting Rob in. "The fuzz, they're going to the bunker! Someone has grassed!"

Rob looked furious. "Which little bastard was it? I'll kill 'im when I find out. They couldn't find it any other way unless someone squealed." They both sat on the baggy sofa and lit up. Better tell Billie in case he's going up there today." The same idea crossed their minds. What if Billie was already there?

"Nah, I saw him going off on the school bus" this morning, said Eddie. "And what were you doing up at eight in the morning?" Rob grinned. "Coming home, what else? But I'm not telling you who I was with." Rob went to grab Eddie's T shirt but missed and fell on the floor. They both laughed it off. "Come on get dressed and we'll go to the bus stop for the bus at 4pm."

Penny and Mark followed the beaten track, now dusty and bare in the summer heat. They followed it to the middle of the airstrip and Mark whistled. "Wow look at that. I never knew this was here, it's a mile long or more!" Penny covered her eyes with a hand, "I suppose there is no need to come here. It's part of the farm land but it's too much trouble to dig it up. I suppose you would be trespassing legally but I doubt the farmer cares."

They moved to the left where a bare patch suggested there had been a hangar years before. They walked up and down and saw that a big patch of brambles and a stunted tree hid the path from the estate. It was clear now there was another path coming from the flats straight to this site. "Here, look, the path is worn away this side of the brambles, and yes, a doorway set down in the mound with a big hole at the side!" Mark shouted.

Chapter Ten

Squire Martyn returns

THE HOUSEHOLD WELCOMED spring with a great deal more humour than the previous year. Rebecca was refreshed by not having to repulse her husband again and again; the servants benefited from her milder temper. Her husband was less intoxicated and more communicative with his children and shouted less at Daniel so that he became less precocious and more able to play and attend his sisters. Benoit and Miss Friend were more able to discharge their duties and altogether the benefits fell on Suzannah too. By March the snow had drifted away, it was easier to wash and dress and keep warm in the great stone manor house and the lengthening of the days saw the sheep lambing in great quantity. The fields began to shimmer in pale green, the hares boxing in the meadows and the roads open to travel.

Suzannah was the only one paying for all this pleasantness by serving her master well. From their initial bargaining point when Squire Martyn seemed satisfied with a brisk fumbling or frottilation, Suzannah began to feel the lack of some essential which she felt by rights was hers and increasingly craved more interaction than she dared admit.

One day when feeding a calf in the stables, Maria and Catherine being at studies, he upped her skirt as usual and aroused himself at her rump when Suzannah involuntarily put her hand down and pushed him inside herself. She was surprised at the sharp pain she felt but more desperate to fulfil her fantasies which were now keeping her awake at night. She gasped at the sensation and held him inside her for some moments all the while grasping at his coat with her hands behind her. Knowing he had now ensnared her desire he stayed for another joust and this time she knew what others craved and sold their souls for.

So did she have him or did he have her? Before he left she sidled against him.

"Sir, you may take your pleasure as you wish as you are my master, but it would show what a gentleman you are if you would grace me with some favours".

"And what would a pretty little maid need that I don't already provide for you?"

"I want to see Bristow". He was now taken aback. Lace, trinkets, gowns even he expected but what had the girl got into her head now?

"Bristow is a bustling, busy place full of sinners and treachery. Why would you want to go there?" She glanced up at him. "I would like to see how more worldly people live. I have never been outside Worsley before and I long to know what the rest of this country is like. Mr Timms spoke of the Indies and the Gold Coast and I should like to see a blackamoor".

Squire Martyn grinned. "A blackamoor? And what prey do you think he would think of you-so slight and golden? Do you not think he would eat you up?"

"I am sure he would not Sir! Ladyship's sister spoke of them and she is no more robust or less attractive than me. She spoke of them with pity."

"Pity!" he gasped, "She can only have had the merest glimpse from afar. No one hawks their wife around the slave market. Anyway how could I take a servant girl to Bristow? How could I explain that away?"

"By taking all your family Sir. Mr Fenwick and his wife are in Bristow and I heard them implore her ladyship to come and visit their fine house, or the Gurneys in Bath will be pleased to accommodate the family. I hear that is not so far from Bristow that we could not visit. I shall be so disappointed Sir if I do not go and may take ill at the loss." She looked up through her dark gold eyelashes and hitched her skirt to show her ankles as she stepped out of the barn. The hint was not lost on Squire Martyn. No trip to Bristow no willing partner.

It was as lent began in March that Squire Martyn announced that once the Easter festivities were over he intended showing off his family in Bristow and had acquired an invitation from Mr Fenwick to stay a fortnight there. Mr Fenwick had much business between the Gold coast and Bristow, bringing in commodities and taking slaves to the West Indies, sailing them out to the colonies again. He had no title or connections but was one of the wealthier tradesmen in Bristow and enjoyed flaunting his wealth. He had built a grand mansion away from the miasma and stews of the city and was set to landscape the many acres as he had heard was fashionable in other great houses. He relished the idea of showing off his plans the draughtsman was still preparing and indicating to his city peers that he was associated with old money. Squire Martyn was nothing to him, an old fashioned and barely educated sot but he did have very good connections in London, some said with the chamber at St James. He had no difficulty offering hospitality to his family for a mere two weeks if it meant some favour in return.

Rebecca was taken aback at her husband's suggestion. "Why William, we hardly know the Fenwicks and I am not sure my constitution will stand the putrefaction of the city". "Be calm Rebecca. The Fenwicks live way out of the city, in the countryside and have several comfortable carriages in which we can travel as far as we choose. You will feel most at home with Mrs Fenwick as you did here and they have a well appointed house with many servants. They are obliged to return the compliment of hospitality that we showed them. I will hear none of it. The day after Easter we travel to Bristow. Make arrangements with the servants"

Rebecca and the girls were to travel in the carriage along with Suzannah. Daniel had been so outraged at being included in the women's party Squire Martyn agreed he could start the journey on his pony knowing he would be dropping with exhaustion after a few hours. It was thirty five miles and if they set off early they could make the inn at Yate by lunchtime. From there they had to travel into the centre of Bristow, down into the Avon Gorge then cross the stone bridge to the other bank where their hosts servants would meet them and guide them to Ashleigh Hall, the Fenwick's new abode.

Suzannah sent word through a servant to her family asking if a little money could be spared for spending in the town. She knew that Squire Martyn would be obliged to meet any bills she incurred but it would look suspicious if she did not ask at home. She was not fearful of plundering her family's wealth. For all their lowliness they were well provided for and the farm made a good profit now the cost of wool was reaching high prices in the low countries. Her father sent back a purse of five shillings, the equivalent of a months earnings at the Manor. Her family wanted her to prosper.

Lent was long and arduous. Rebecca took her devotions seriously; prayed three times a day, did not eat any red meat or fowl and ensured the girls were similarly deprived. Suzannah felt relieved, the fare at the manor was far richer than she was used to at home and the simple dishes of grain and eggs and vegetables suited her well enough. Squire Martyn ignored his wife's reproaches. He went out hunting as usual, returning with pheasant and hares as he wished and consumed as much red wine as he liked. His initial lust for Suzannah had abated now she was colluding with him and he spent days away at other gentlemen's houses, no doubt indulging his appetites for other sports in the bull pit and cockpits of Gloucestershire.

Eventually Easter was over and the servants began loading garments and toiletries for the family's sojourn. Suzannah had to be careful not to let them touch her chest and find the vinegar, so said she would pack her own clothes. She wore her blue dress and packed her second best gown and linen. Squire Martyn had given her lambskin gloves, a mother of pearl clasp for her hair and some beads made of jet that she was not to show to Rebecca. She intended that in Bristow he should do better by her and her old gown could be left behind for the poor.

She climbed into the carriage with Rebecca, Maria and Catherine, her hair styled in a formal plait of gold around her head and a starched bonnet of creamy linen with a blue ribbon threaded through. Around her throat she wore a single pearl on a chain and when Rebecca asked, told her an uncle had brought it back for her and sent it to her at Christmas. Squire Martyn had given it to her after their first copulation and they agreed the story to dupe Rebecca. She would not have any discourse with Suzannah's mother. On her hands she wore the lambskin gloves and about her the expensive scent he had given her only that week. Rebecca looked at her with consternation.

"Miss Garrod, I know it is the custom for servants to make the best of themselves when in company but it would be in keeping if you presented yourself less costly than your charge." Suzannah nodded obediently but secretly smiled out of the corner of her mouth as she looked out of the carriage window. Rebecca had yet to see the lengths to which Suzannah intended to flaunt herself.

The journey was hideous. They bumped along the local lanes, pot-holed from winter snows and Suzannah began to feel nauseous before they reached the High Road. But reach it they did and by nine am the horses were briskly making their way along a sturdier route peopled by other carriages and horsemen. A handsome young man on a large chestnut rode by and doffed his cap. Rebecca, who on her side had the cover down, was shocked to see Suzannah acknowledge him with a nod of the head and a lengthy glance, but she said nothing. The girl was fifteen now and if she chose to flaunt herself she would be out of a job before long. She would speak to her in the privacy of the Fenwick's home, out of earshot of Maria.

Suzannah recognising she had overstepped the mark, pulled the cover down half way.

"Why Madam, it is startling to have strangers staring at one from every direction. I see why you travel unnoticed."

Yet she did not pull the cover down completely. After three hours they stopped at the Inn at Yate, a furious place with carriages back and forth across the cobbles, servants scurrying hither and thither, piles of ordure from the horses unattended and all manner of people lounging around the streets. Suzannah was quite scared, held on tight to her purse and waited until the footman had brought the box for her to alight from. Squire Martyn had called a boy over who laid some sacks across the path to the inn door and he had secured private rooms upstairs whence they retired. There was a low ceilinged sitting room looking over the street and a bedroom and closet to which she quickly repaired with Maria. Once refreshed they sat in the window seat to see the activities below which she found fascinating. A red faced man was trying to sell trinkets to customers, whittled whistles, snuff boxes, pegs and tooth picks. He had little luck and Suzannah thought all for the better as he looked as consumed by strong drink as Squire Martyn usually was.

A small boy with one leg and a rough crutch begged for money, but got very little. Another coach approached and two fine young women alighted, with brimmed hats, and descended on the preferred sacking, tossing groats to the lame boy. They did not come upstairs but were accompanied by a servant. Suzannah took note of their costumes and accessories and thought "that is how I will dress one day. The coach was high and black and had black horses. It picked up parcels all logged in a book and stowed on top of the roof.

Their own two horses were tired but were to go on with them to Bristow. They had to wait two hours for the horses to be fed, watered and rested. Squire Martyn stayed in the public part of the inn exchanging information with the other travellers and drinking more than necessary. The women and Daniel remained closeted upstairs. Miss Friend had not been invited and Rebecca was to be given the services of a ladies maid at Ashleigh Hall so Suzannah was the only servant who travelled with her. She was therefore obliged to attend to her needs and make a comfortable bed for her to rest on once they had eaten. The food was good if solid. A steak pie followed by baked apples and curds. Plain good food she would recognise in her own home.

At last they were on their way again. Daniel was persuaded to come into the carriage and sat between his mother and Catherine while Maria and Suzannah had the bench to themselves. The road was straight and increasingly sloped towards the south until they could see the shining sea to their right, reflecting pale blue in the spring sunshine. As they neared the city they were aware of the smoke and fumes from myriad chimneys, foundries and fuller's works, leather makers, a thousand putrid trades poured their effluent into the air until the blue of the sea and sky disappeared behind grey shoulders of land blotted out by pollution. Alongside the road lay rough cottages and hamlets, turning to brick buildings with pools of foetid water alongside the road. The road became paved at one point and they were checking the horses to make their way down a long slow slope. Before it steepened they were excited to see the workshops had given way to high buildings, housing little shops with open fronts selling everything from baskets to blankets. Ribbons, hats, fabrics, shawls, metalware, tools, saddlery, food and shops with butchers and dairy produce, gun shops and tailors. There was too much to look at and Maria and Catherine moved from side to side of the carriage to glimpse each new view. Suzannah kept her dignity and sat back so as not to draw attention to herself. They now had Daniel with them so were more crowded and he showed more decorum than the girls.

The route through the city seemed endless. Eventually the variety of shops and houses, the sights and the signs wearied them and they sat back listless as the carriage pulled up a shallow incline on to the river margin and its quays. At the narrowest point of the river was a broad span of stone bridge above which the ships could not sail and they could not resist pulling up the cloth covers to look over the edge into the swirling waters. Below, the wharves were endless with boats of all sizes pulled into the quays and an endless stream of packages carried and lifted from the boats to the quays. Beyond the sparkling water widened out to flow between two huge promontories of rock, hundreds of feet above the gorge. Inside the gorge, the warehouses continued and the mass of people and bodies was as indistinguishable on the land as those who hauled and pushed the cargos on the boats. The carriage eventually reached the far side of the bridge and then the horses were hard pushed to start their long ascent to the upper reaches of Ashleigh Park. This last part of the journey seemed endless, and although the equinox was passed it was already darkling when they arrived at the Hall greeted by Mr and Mrs Fenwick. Suzannah no longer felt crisp and smart. She was tired and dirty from the fumes, no longer fragrant and she longed to bathe herself in private to remove the grime of the journey. Fortunately the Fenwicks kept plenty of servants and their luggage was dispatched to their respective rooms; Maria and Suzannah were able to withdraw in privacy with a young maidservant to tend to their hair and provide washing facilities. Suzannah took easily to being waited upon and asked the maid to take away their linen and changed to clean before putting on their dresses and shoes again. They soon felt well enough for company and at seven o'clock went downstairs to join their elders for dinner. It was a formal affair. Numerous dishes were presented and wine was made available for all although Rebecca declined on behalf of her daughters and Suzannah. Before long the gentlemen went to another room and the ladies to the parlour and the girls were sent up to their rooms. "My Suzannah, how far we have come today!" said Maria wide eyed.

"Yes we have come far" said Suzannah not referring to the length of their journey.

In the morning the Fenwicks arranged a gentle ride around the park in an open carriage. The weather was bright with showers threatening by lunchtime so they cut their journey short and spent the afternoon indoors. Suzannah was at a loss not having her embroidery or books to turn to and Catherine spending much of her time with Rebecca. She was not considered old enough or important enough to join in the conversation but neither could she go out on her own. In the evening they had invited some local neighbours to visit and to meet Squire Martyn and his wife. The girls were told they would meet the guests but would dine early and then go to their rooms before dinner was served. Suzannah was mortified. She had not come all this way to be sent to her room and be ushered away like a child. She wanted to meet people and find out how they lived in a city so different from country life where the conversation was only about beasts and crops and weather. She would be sixteen in summer, ready to marry. How should she meet anyone apart from the blacksmiths son?

They spent the early evening indoors and Maria was shown a handsome spinette in the main hall of the house. They amused themselves looking at new music and practicing some songs. At six they were ushered upstairs to prepare for guests. Suzannah changed into her velvet gown. Her old one looked awful next to the Fenwicks rich clothes and the guests' gowns would be even more sumptuous. Nevertheless her blue would have to do and she put on a white lace cap over her golden braids and the pearl chain. She showed the maid servant how to wind Maria's hair and did Catherine's herself. Maria had a deep red wool dress with silver lace at collar and cuffs and a ruby brooch at the neck. Catherine's was pale green satin. As a group they descended the staircase and the gathered adults were impressed. They curtseyed nicely and when Suzannah looked up there was Robert Timms admiring her. She gasped a little, not less because when she previously met him she had been a virgin and wholesome. Now she could hardly bear to look him in the face.

Timms was pleasant enough to her but she noticed he kept himself available to be amiable to all the other women in the room. There were two merchants, one a dutchman and his wife. Mrs Fenwick's sister and her husband and another young man called Deake made up the party. He looked far less comfortable than Timms and Suzannah amused herself by approaching him and asking what he did in the world. He was a clerk to the dutch merchant, much travelled it seemed, and was about to sail to the Dutch East Indies.

"We are growing spice plantations in the Dutch indies" he said solemnly "and my job is to ensure our gang masters are utilising the local natives effectively. They become lazy and do not instil discipline and morality in their charges. Then the natives revolt and we lose production. We have to keep a tight ship".

Suzannah wondered what and where the Dutch Indies might be and asked lots of questions about how far away and how big were the islands. She was amazed to discover that it took three months to sail there in good weather and good fortune and could only be undertaken at certain times of the year because of the winds that would drive the ships. She wondered if Timms would be going away for so many months. It was not too hard to play the guileless child amongst grownups as Maria and Catherine did it to perfection. The Dutch man was much taken with Catherine's dark looks and smiled and pinched her cheek. Suzannah began to see that all men were lecherous. She supposed Squire Martyn was probably no different from all the others in such worldly places.

After an hour or so, when she had had little opportunity to engage Timms on his own, they were ushered out of the room and their maid brought them broth and bread to their room where they all sat in candle light and retold all the stories they each had heard from the merchants. The other man was a slave merchant like Fenwick. Maria said that he brought blackamoors to Barbados to be bought and sold like cattle.

"How can you sell a man?" Suzannah queried. "Surely he owns himself. Why would they allow themselves to be sold?"

"Oh Mr Fenwick says the King of the Gold Coast catches them there in wars and they are prisoners. He would kill them otherwise so being a slave means at least you get to live. And Mr Fenwick says the work they do in Virginia is very easy in the plantations".

Suzannah tried to imagine if her father or uncle were captured and taken half way round the world by strangers whether they would feel grateful for the privilege. To be taken away from your home and family forever and not know your fate and work for only your food and shelter must be a horrible existence, she thought. It would be more noble to be killed in battle than be caught. "We shall see them tomorrow" said Catherine nonchalantly. "There is a cargo come in today and tomorrow the slaves will be paraded on the quay for the gang masters to choose. We are to go and watch".

Suzannah was taken aback at Catherine's lack of compassion as if she were discussing animals and she only ten years old. She wondered if the girls had been fed this type of language by their father all their lives leading to a general callousness in the whole family. No wonder Rebecca was so reluctant to come here. But this is what Suzannah had come to see, Bristow and all its workings and activities. If she married someone from here like Timms she would have to become as cynical and cold as the inhabitants had become and would be living off the slave trade and its atrocities.

Suzannah read from the prayer book before they went to sleep and to thank God for their good fortune in having wealth and a generous father and mother to take care of them. She slept soundly knowing Squire Martyn would not risk impropriety in another man's house.

Day broke and they were pleased to see it was fair and bright. The girls were up early, groomed and presented in their best finery and after a meal of porridge and dried fruits climbed into the carriage. The horses were fresh and pranced all the way down to the environs of the docks. Martyn and Fenwick rode their best horses looking grand and wealthy. As far as she could see there were the towering masts of the tall ships, their sails furled, bobbing about the swell of the Avon as the tide came up the river. The industry was furious, youths ran from warehouse to wharf collecting bales of tobacco, spices, sugar, silk and other fabrics. Outgoing were giant bales of wool and cloth, coal and ore. The sailors were cleaning the decks and attending to the rigging, the stevedores carrying great loads on to the ships and manhandling ropes and pulleys to get ballast aboard.

The carriage slowed and turned along the quayside and Mr Fenwick, from his horse, pointed out one of his ships, The Betty. "That is one of mine", he bragged. "She is unloading from Virginia and will set sail to the Gold Coast by the next tide. This my latest ship, made to carry 500 slaves in one journey. There is such a dearth of black slaves since the rebellion in '76 we cannot get enough of them." His smug grin made Suzannah wince. "Surely Sir, these men are just as we are, they have their sorrows and ambitions as white men do?"

"Poor child, she does not know any better! Do you not know the rebellion was by white slaves not black. The blacks are used to the heat and find working in the Indies so much more amenable to their stature than men from Europe. They are not free men, they are prisoners of war. For centuries their brothers in Barbary captured white men all the way up the English channel. Have you never read your Pepys? The story of Reverent Devereux Spratt? Captured and suffered for twelve years in Egypt? We are only carrying on their heinous trade."

Suzannah felt crushed. She did not know the story he spoke of and it was not her place to argue with her host, but she felt there was something inherently wrong with his attitude. She hoped some Barbary corsair would capture Mr Fenwick and Squire Martyn one day so they would see the suffering first hand.

On the quay a stone building stood with barred windows. Outside, a scaffold platform stood where the slaves were displayed. She could see from a distance their ebony skin and tall frames against the whitened wall. The carriage pulled up and nearby Mr Fenwick made his way through the crowd, to where the slave master stood showing off his wares. Squire Martyn leaned across, "They will sell the best slaves here, see that man on the end? He will be a prize for some master." Suzannah was shocked to see their feet were shackled, one to the other, and they were prodded with sticks and caned if they did not move fast enough. A woman and a boy were manacled together, a youth looked thin and weak but was described as placid. Then came a Trojan of a man, barely dressed, his torso rippled with muscle. She gasped at the prospect of such a powerful man being herded like an animal. His legs were cut where the metal trussed his ankles, and in his face she saw the image of his destroyed soul. To be paraded in front of this rabble, someone who would have been revered and ennobled in his own country, shamed her into tears.

Martyn leaned across again, "Since the King gave the Charter to the Company of Adventurers we cannot sell or trade slaves but we Bristowmen do not worry about trivial legislation. We have trade to make!" Suzannah felt sickened and searched for her kerchief. How could the likes of Timms and Fenwick be party to this monstrous trade? How could they swagger and joke about the misery inflicted on these people? This was the business that Martyn was in and which brought his wealth, his money, his jewels and spices. Now she was also party to it and felt mortified. Maria picked up her mood and looked crestfallen. She pulled at the blind on the carriage. "Father," she begged, "can we move on please?" Her father and Fenwick, smiled at each other. "Such pity the young bear in their breasts" he smirked. Mr Fenwick looked disdainful. "Perhaps they would disembark and examine the goods close up! Then they would appreciate why these captives must be chained." He was clearly affronted by their distaste.

The carriage was taken further along the quay before they could turn and on return Suzannah saw the eyes of the tall man on her, his hatred burning into her retreating presence. They turned over the bridge to the town and the girls descended and were escorted by servants among the stalls and shops of the northern slopes. Rebecca had taken a back seat in the carriage and had not looked out at the quays. She now examined leather gloves, hosiery and fabric. She made her purchases while the servant paid the coin. Suzannah was stunned by the variety of products on offer. The fabrics were extraordinary, the colours vibrant and glossy compared to the dull stuff they were used to see traded by journeymen at home. Maria begged for some emerald silk but was refused; Catherine wanted deep gold but was told that was for titled persons only. Rebecca reminded them that it was against God's will to expose oneself flamboyantly and vanity was a sin; nevertheless she looked and looked herself at the bounty.

Suzannah did not ask for anything but was provided with deep blue velvet and she caught sight of Martyn smirking and winking behind his wife's back. She was shocked by Rebecca's matter of fact manner but Rebecca was brisk about her purchase. "That will suit you very well Suzannah, we cannot have you in shabby attire if you are to mix in company." Rebecca bustled about and the girls likewise got crimson and deep plum velvet. "I will get it made up for you at home," Rebecca said nonchalantly. The girls peered at lace and trinkets which were haggled over by the servant. They entered a bootmakers and all came out better shod in fine leather than when they went in. Rebecca bought herself a silver chatelaine and ivory beads carved in Cathay. Suzannah was amazed at the luxury of such goods and how Rebecca could afford such fripperies. No doubt Squire Martyn had bid her make a show of their wealth to impress the Fenwicks as Rebecca was unlikely to wear anything other than her lace cap and black attire only cheered by her coral ring.

They returned to Ashleigh House after refreshing themselves at an Inn and, ensuring all the parcels were on board. Suzannah should have been excited but she could not wipe away the accusing gaze of the black man in the market. He had looked straight at her. How must it have looked coming in all their wealth to stare on his humiliation.

Squire Martyn rode back with them. "How does Miss Garrod like her new purchases?" he enquired. She knew this was her payment for her favours yet to come. "Well enough Sir, her ladyship has been very generous to me." She knew very well Rebecca had been instructed to buy the clothes and to give her the benefit of generosity was to rile him. "I am sure you will look very fine in your new livery," he said as he ran his hand against her thigh as the others turned to enter the house.

That evening they entertained the local parson and his wife as well as a neighbor from nearby Pill. It was quite a different evening from the night before. Sober and sombre and Maria was invited to play sacred music on the spinette so Suzannah was permitted to stay later. As she left the drawing room Squire Martyn appeared from a corridor and seized her. "And now my beauty, we will need to have a little plan for tonight!" She looked uncomprehendingly at him. "You don't think those gifts are free do you?"

She hedged a while. "It is a strange house. I do not know my way about." He drew nearer, squeezing her buttock. "When you go to bed with Maria make some excuse to get water or something and I will meet you in the servant's stairwell." She stammered, "there is a maid Sir, to fetch water, I cannot leave the room." "Then send her away. I cannot wait days for you to play me around."

Suzannah was afraid. He meant to get his reward and for her it was easier to give in for a few moments than refuse. If she made a commotion her behavior would be exposed and she would be shamed in a foreign house and sent home. She could not face that, her parents knowing her descent into debauchery.

When they had finished their toilette she told the maid she would see to Maria's hair herself. She then went to the closet and soaked her sponge in vinegar. She tipped the ewer over and exclaimed "Oh Maria I have spilled the water. I must get more for the morning." She slipped down the servant's stair and found Martyn lurking there in the dark. He grabbed her elbow and pulled her into a closet full of laundry. She put down her ewer but he was already pulling at her skirts and unbuttoning his breeches. She was now used to this and braced herself on the smooth, cold stone of the wall. It was over quickly. She mused how well cut was the stonework of this new building compared to the rough walls of the manor. She counted the sheets at her feet and wondered if they were sent out for washing. Martyn was drunk and after a brief stab of pain he was grunting and released her soon. Once she felt she was free of him she grabbed her ewer and went in search of the scullery. She was becoming immune to her degradation.

She washed carefully before going to bed in fear that Maria would sense the odour of a man on her. By the time she crept beneath the sheet Maria was fast asleep. How beautiful to be so innocent and safe, she mused.

The days proceeded. They did not go back to the docks. A recurring vision came to her mind, when she was not occupied, of the pitiable state of the man in the market.

She began to feel that marriage to anyone in Bristow who could tolerate such horrors would be unbearable and began dreaming of the curate and the blacksmiths son as a potential future for her. But who would want a soiled woman for wife?

Guests came to view the visitors. Although Rebecca was closeted in a rural backwater, Martyn was clearly famous in his own field. She met young men; solemn ones, cheerful ones, lecherous ones. She was described as the childrens' governess, although it was Miss Friend who actually taught them, not her. Her height and strong frame made her seem older than her charge so no one questioned her abilities and as she could read and write, translate a little Latin and read music she passed well enough.

Squire Martyn came to her every night. The Fenwicks had provided a single room for the Martyn's which must have disgusted Rebecca, but she showed no sign of repulsion or distress. In some ways Suzannah hoped her own suffering was protecting Rebecca from the most brutal impositions of her husband. She wondered if Rebecca guessed what was happening, right under her nose, and supposed if exposed she would be thrown out. Or perhaps not. Rebecca would not want the scandal exposed and it suited her well for Martyn's lusts to be quenched elsewhere with a girl she could manage and control. Buying that blue velvet must have sickened her.

All too soon the fortnight was over. They had been invited to two houses in the district and Suzannah had caught the eye of at least one or two sons of merchants. Timms had been pleasant and attentive as before but there had been no progress in their communication. After considering his vocation and need to please his master she was less inclined to throw herself in his path. If business meant destroying other men's souls maybe she was not cut out to be a merchants wife after all. She watched the other women; wives, mothers; they seemed so compliant and complacent about about slave trading as if the poor creatures were not even human. Were they oblivious to death and suffering in others? She decided it was a subject she could only discuss with her own kind.

Being in Bristow and near Bath they had arranged to visit the Gurneys. They resided in a small town house with a long domain behind where grain was stored. It was a relief to be in the company of decent people again. Sarah Gurney was full of talk about fashion and society and her husband Charles was excited to explain the plans they had for their son Richard who was becoming a scholar, the first in their family.

Their fare was much more to Suzannah's taste, good plain food with small beer compared with the rich, indigestible dishes at the Fenwicks.

The talk was all of plague. It had been destroyed in London twenty years since after the Great Fire but due to the docks at Plymouth and Bristow seemed to rally and reappear where there was squalor and overcrowding. As Bath was on the main thoroughfare from Bristow to London Sarah Gurney was convinced some merchant would pass through and start another outbreak in Bath as they had seen last year. All around the house were bunches of sage and cloths soaked in lavender water at the doors and windows, which were shut tight even though the heat was high for April.

"Pray Sarah, if you are so fearful please come and stay with us until the danger is over. We have plenty of space for you all and I am sure Suzannah will help with the little one.

The air is pure and fresh and we have so few visitors there is no fear of contamination. We would be pleased to offer you hospitality in these worrying times."

Mrs Gurney was grateful but she could not see how, with her son at school in the town and her husbands business, that they could remove to another county. But the offer was there. They only stayed two nights and were off again along the Malmesbury road this time, back to Worsley Hall.

Within three weeks Suzannah's dress was made up, fitted and put in the gardrobe for future wear. After the ostentation of Bristow Suzannah wondered wherever she would be able to wear it. She kept her old grey wool dress for undertaking chores, with the servants and wore her blue wool dress for daytimes. In addition Squire Martyn had purchased her some exquisite beads called lapis which he said had been brought from Constantinople, a place she could not imagine. The stories Benoit told made it seem like an imaginary place in the heavens rather than just another port like Bristow. She knew there were other gems far finer but even Rebecca only had one stone in her ring other than the pearls in her locket. On one or two occasions Suzannah had slipped into Rebeccas room and looked at her dresser and its fine brushes and jewel case. She began to fantasise about how Squire Martyn could be further manipulated to give her finer items. But also she began to fantasise about how he may take more trouble to pleasure her rather than just fumble at her rump, leaving her unsatisfied.

It was May and the weather was being kind to the land, engendering crops and food was plenty. The ponies were frisky when they rode out and Catherine often went out leaving Suzannah behind. Daniel was always practicing his fencing these days and so Suzannah decided to make a tryst with the Squire in the barn. He could order the stable boy away and cheerily waved off the girls on their ponies. Suzannah was hiding in a stall and loosened her gown so that when Squire Martyn appeared in the doorway she let it slip to the ground, allowing him to remove her petticoats. She had irresistable pale skin and long slender legs and it was soon the Squire was able to feast his lust on her exposed beauty. Suzannah lay back in the hay and tried to enjoy the sensation. At least he did not smell and he had not been drinking so hard since they returned from Bath. He had once been a handsome man, she could see that, but his frame was bloated with excesses in drink and food and his face now was sagging and flabby. She closed her eyes and tried to imagine him as his portrait in the hall showed him. She stared up at the rafters as he floundered above her.

"Child you have bewitched me with your ways. No woman should have such soft skin and golden curls. Your titties are like ripe apples and I cannot keep my hands from your body. The Good Lord should not tempt a man with such glories if he wishes him to be moral and devout. You are nothing but a whore but I would put aside my wife and recognize you in public." Suzannah was alarmed. The last she wanted was to be exposed as a whore to her family. "Sir, it could destroy your business and humiliate your children to do so. How much better to enjoy the fruit of love in secret and have our trysts as and when we wish. You can thank me in many ways other than the censure of the world." He leered at her. "You are a clever little vixen. I knew as soon as I saw you in church I should have you. You slut, you Jezebel".

Calling her names seemed to rouse him more and he was able to take her again and again until she was shent with lust. She began to feel her own desire rising in her and clasping her legs around him gave vent to her fulfillment with a scream. Suddenly she did not mind how she looked or who should discover them, her own desire seemed to rid her of any sensibilities. She was disturbed to see how smug he looked as he hooked his breeches back again and Suzannah realised she had now succumbed to a role of subservience and he now had the upper hand.

Squire Martyn made no attempt to go away that summer. He lingered in the house, made fewer trips to gaming events and even drank less at dinner. Almost every day he maneuvered the household so that Suzannah was often alone. They coupled in closets and cupboards and on one occasion even in Maria's bed in the daytime. He seemed careless of discovery and Suzannah was sure some of the servants had spied on them but if Rebecca had not been convinced at Bristow by the purchase of the blue velvet she showed no sign of spite against Suzannah. No doubt Martyn's sobriety and cheerfulness and lack of attention to her suited her happily.

Suzannah was now able to command money for her services. She could not possess anymore jewels and finery without promoting suspicion in the household and now had a locked box of her own. She demanded silver, incense, perfumes and the best linen and accoutrements for her person, but the money meant more to her. She had amassed about a years' wages, separate from her earnings for being a servant and she was wondering if she should start planning a future for herself. She realized that Squire Martyn would resent any attempt of hers to marry elsewhere even if she succeeded in alluring some other man and would not tolerate losing "his little golden whore" as he called her.

In the summer she was able to spend time with her family and was again in communion with her sister Constance. "Suzannah, you no longer fret about Squire Martyn's lechery. Has he stopped pestering you?" Suzannah said nothing then looked helplessly at her sister. "Suzannah, he has tupped you, hasn't he?" Constance raised her hands to her face in horror. "Hasn't he! I can tell from your face. There is a sense of knowledge about you that was not there before."

"Constance, please do not despise me. I could not see how I could refuse him. It is my job. I was not so fortunate as you to be made an offer of marriage and must find my way as best I can." Constance hugged her. "You are not with child then?" "No sister; I use the vinegar as you told me." Constance looked in shock. "As I told you! I did not think you would need it for yourself. You are only sixteen, still time to find a husband but how will you explain your condition when you are broken?" Suzannah had hardened her heart by now. "I shall have to find a man as enamoured of me as Squire Martyn is or as ignorant of what to expect as a child."

It was only on declaring the truth that Suzannah acknowledged the corruption into which she had fallen. However must Constance view her now as a common whore. She had not even dared to say she was being paid for her favours. At least she had enough money to set herself up in business if all else failed, maybe in Bath where her history could not be guessed at. She thought maybe she could set up a linen shop and take in sewing and mending or even employ others. But she could not face being separated from her family and them knowing her shame.

The weather was hot and humid. The corn was being gathered in but the grain was damp and needed threshing and drying to prevent moulding. Suzannah languished indoors where the cool thick stone walls contained the cool air. She had two days with her family then had to return to Worsley Hall because Rebecca was ailing again. She clung on to Constance on leaving and nothing more was said between them again. She knew Constance would keep her secret and if she was got with child at least one person would not need an explanation.

Chapter Eleven

The Bunker

MARK BENSON AND Penny Worstham levered aside the metal door pushing back the brambles. From a few feet away it looked derelict, as if no one ever came there. Once you got up to it you could see the soil was flattened by boots and the door edge was smooth and shiny from handling, the brambles snapped off. Mark shone his torch inside.

"Blimey, it goes down a bit. They must be desperate for some privacy down here."

Detecting the ladder Mark put one leg in and gave Penny the torch. Once they were in they could see it was less derelict than they thought. Several plastic beer crates were lying around and a couple of old car seats. A pile of magazines, well-thumbed were on a crate in the corner and there were a variety of bits of foil, bottles and other obscure objects used for drugs. Beer cans and bottles were strewn around leaving a stale sour smell in the shuttered gloom.

Mark shone his torch around. The walls were concrete sleepers laid one on top of the other. At the bottom they were shuttered with ply wood panels that were rotten with damp and at the back wall one had been replaced with an old door. The floor appeared to be beaten earth. He shone the torch around again; nothing exceptional, he flicked through the magazines; nothing unexpected, no children or pets. In fact nothing but a boy's den.

They hauled themselves out of the bunker and radioed in to report very little and to arrange for the repair crew to come and seal up the door and padlock it shut. Mark wondered who owned the hangar and aerodrome.

"If it's the RAF they should come and fill it in once and for all. It's a health hazard." Penny winked at him, "Well the magazines are!"

They strolled back across the aerodrome in sunlight and got back into the car. Penny was thinking, "we could have found another body in there, didn't think about it really did we?"

Mark squinted through the sunbeams, "you're right, where drugs are concerned anything is possible. Funny after all this time we've had no problems before; why now? What has changed in the last month that would introduce plague into the estate-it's crazy."

Alice Best, drugs worker, sat in Frankie's living room trying to be matter of fact about HIV and Hep C. She had picked up from Helen Bourne that there was more to Frankie's mental state than drugs but did not want to alarm her so stuck to the initial discussions around harm reduction in drug use.

"The symptoms of Hep C are a bit like flu, fever, headache, weakness. If you think you have had a bout like that its worth getting it checked out by your doctor. The earlier it's treated the less damage it can cause. Oh and you'd need to be careful about alcohol too."

Frankie was staring ahead not taking in what she was saying.

"Frankie, I feel I'm missing something. You look scared but nothing I'm saying is reassuring you. We can fix this you know."

Frankie turned huge frightened eyes towards her. "Do you believe in ghosts?"

Before Alice could reply Frankie went on to a garbled monologue.

"Jake said after people die and get buried they can wake up and walk about- like zombies. If something horrible had happened to them like murder. That's why he was always saying he wanted to be burned after he died. He said those zombies could come back and haunt the people who hurt them but if you were strong you could get control over them by mind control and make them do things for you."

"Frankie, you know all that is rubbish. Fairy tales for children. He just wanted to scare people. That's how he controlled others and that is why he hung out with young ones. No adults would listen to that twaddle."

There was a glimmer of hope in Frankie's eyes. Alice went on, "never has anyone found any proof at all ever anywhere that people come back from the dead. It's just movie stories and fantasy."

"So what killed Jake? He said he knew where a body was buried that would make him rich and then he was killed."

"Heroin most likely. This scare about plague is probably some mistake. It's a virus or something that looks like it.

There are wild animals that carry a form of plague, in California for instance, maybe Jake got bitten by a bat."

This conjured up more livid pictures of Jake as Dracula but Frankie did not make the connection. She quietened down visibly in Alice's calm presence.

"Why can't her mother do this?" thought Alice. "She wouldn't have gone on to drugs if she had had a sensitive adult around. She gave Frankie some literature on safe sex and went.

Outside the block where Jake had died was decorated with a different colour tape; environmental health. Everyone in the block had been moved to hotels, and tests were being done on all the flats, drains, walls, doors, extractor fans and pets to see if there was any evidence of the plague. In the meantime the three flats next to Jake's had happy tenants; single men who had hated being stuck out in Worsley, were now in Gloucester, albeit in a shabby B and B but next to the pubs and clubs they enjoyed.

Two single mothers were staying with relatives not wanting to cope with the kids in a hotel. All of them hoped the Council would close them down and rehouse them in some bright well decorated estates near Gloucester.

Billy came in from Marj McCormack's. His mother Evie had been a victim of abuse by Billy's father who was now in prison for GBH. She was glad. It was worth the monthly visit to Bristow to have 29 other days of peace and quiet. She knew she should have left him at the start but somehow never had the energy. She had missed her chance when he was sent down but she was still scared of what he would do if she left him. It was not fear of assault, he always stopped short of breaking bones, it was weariness and exhaustion from the constant bullying. There had been times she wished he had killed her just to get some peace but she was worried about Billy. She did not know how to share this with him but she knew he had seen more than he should have done, even from a baby. She knew he was a bully at school but she did not mind that, he needed to stand up for himself. Many was the time the teachers had sent him home or suspended him for fighting at school, but now she worried if he would turn on women like his Dad. Billy was very silent about his Dad. They seemed to get on fine but Billy never let much out and she was beginning to notice he was becoming abusive of her, shouting back, telling her to fuck off if she challenged him, as if she was to blame for the poverty and broken furniture not his Dad.

This made her feel even less able to deal with the violence. She did not keep it secret either. The social knew about it, her doctor knew about it and the school now but no one else did anything to help her so she assumed it must be normal. She had two girls as well as Billy. Their Dad had never laid a finger on them and she had believed she was protecting them as long as he only hit her.

"When they're sixteen I'll leave him" she dreamed.

"What's for tea Mum," Billy slumped in front of the T.V. "Sausages" she replied opening the freezer and pulling them out and remembering she had forgotten to get them out. "What sort" he grunted from the living room. "The sausage sort, what else." She was getting annoyed. "I don't want those crap ones we had last week," he grumbled. She tried to remember. What had they had last week? "I'm not made of money you know. You'll have to eat what I can afford now your Dad's inside."

Billy would have used that opportunity to start a row but did not. He did not know why he did it, it just relieved some of the pressure inside him. He did not know where that came from either. It was before Jake's death, before Jake even. He always felt as if he was going to explode. He took it out on kids at school, on the weedy boys, and only the hash with Jake seemed to relieve it or when he was drinking at Marj's but the dope was best. You could get up in the bunker and forget for hours all your worries and pain. He started singing a song from an old record that Jake had. The familiar feeling of abandon and timelessness that Jake had created in the bunker crept back into his mind and he felt his stomach unknot. Maybe those sausages were not that bad.

There was a bang on the door, a fist. Only Billy's friends did that. His two sisters looked out from their bedroom and his mother bawled from the kitchen. "Well answer it then, it's not going to be for me." A voice was coming through the door, "Billy. Billy let me in!" It was Nicky Rowe. Billy got up and let him in and he pushed Billy into his small bedroom next to the front door.

"Bill. They've found it. The police are up there now!" Billy did not need to be told what he meant. He grabbed his denim jacket and went out the door at a lick. Billy's Mum came out of the kitchen, a frying pan of smoking sausages in her hand. "Where are you going now?" she shouted after them.

Penny Worstham had tracked down Annie, Jake's girlfriend. Annie was thirty eight, a sometime heroin user that had somehow got her life together in recent years. She had known Jake for twenty years when they started out in drugs together and there was not much she did not know about him. Penny told her he was dead and she agreed to identify the body at the morgue through glass. On the way there Penny did most of her questioning, using the shock of the death to coerce Annie into saying more than she would otherwise.

"I can't believe it of Jake" she snivelled. Annie looked a tough case, not prone to crying in general. "He was the tough one really, always in control. He never injected but smoked a bit, he never had problems, he took care of himself. And he knew what he was buying too. Had a good nose for a good deal."

Penny purred sympathetically. "You'll miss having him around then?"

"Yeah, when you've done drugs people don't really understand unless they've been there. They don't realise it's on your back all your life. I don't even think about it now thanks to Jake. I've been clean for six years now, for my son, that's the only reason."

Annie spoke of her life, "I have a fifteen year old son in foster care. He had been taken off me at age nine and for two years I only seen him supervised by a social worker once a week. Then I made the decision I didn't want my boy seeing me in that state, got into rehab and stuck to its rules afterwards. My boy was old enough to understand and supported me more than I supported him". Annie's relationship with Jake had therefore been distant as far as the authorities knew. She knew she would never get her boy back if they knew Jake was around. That was why they usually met up in Worsley or other parts of Gloucestershire rather than being seen in the city.

At the morgue she stood back as the gowned and masked assistant pulled back the cloth from Jake's face trying not to reveal the blackened neck. She nodded and moved quickly away. Already Penny could see she was steeling herself to life without her long term friend and confidant, probably her only one. Penny drove her back home and without asking came indoors and saying "I'll make you a coffee."

The flat was tidy and sparse and the most telling factors were the portrait style photos of her son, Kenny, at all ages. Penny did her softening up chat. "He is a good looking lad, Annie. Do you still see his father?" It was clear Kenny was not Jake's at least. He had a round boyish face, smiling grey eyes and fair hair.

"No. His dad was a casual trick I'd guess. I was on skag by then. I only know who he was by the way Kenny looks. Dead spit of his Dad, but I never told him. Some bloke I used to shag for money for brown. He wasn't a user. Liked to tell his mates he hung out with junkies. I expect he is married to some decent woman and Kenny has brothers and sisters somewhere. I was in Cheltenham one day with Kenny looking at shops. I could never afford to buy anything but I saw this kid like Kenny's double. Good job Kenny was looking the other way at the time. I wanted to follow him to see if he was with Kenny's dad but I could not follow with Kenny there. After that I went to Cheltenham every Saturday to try and see him but I couldn't. Kenny would like a brother, but I would never let it happen again after he was born." She stared dismally out of the window, recalling her early life with Kenny in a series of council flats then the private rented bedsits as her circumstances deteriorated until Kenny was taken away from her.

Penny passed her a big mug of coffee. "So how long have you and Jake been together-you know?" "We went to the same school, bunked off together, both got into the drug scene. After Kenny was born I lost touch, but when they took Kenny away I met him at some flat where I was scoring. Somehow he just seemed to be around a lot after that and made me feel familiar and safe. He wasn't a dealer you know. That's what everyone thought."

Penny's mind was working quickly. "But he was a heroin user." "No he used to smoke it occasionally after he went to London in the seventies but he was always with the right people, he looked after them, told them about local stash. There was a right bastard family used to supply. If you didn't pay up in the week they'd do your windows in with baseball bats, then the next time it was your home or your legs." She looked panic stricken at the memory. "Everyone paid. They'd do anything they could to get the money. My boyfriend at that time got five years for burglary to give them their dues, so my flat didn't get done over."

She sipped her coffee like she wanted Penny to stay. She needed to talk to someone now. "Then Jake came on the scene, he'd come back from London and knew a few tricks. He knew people from Birmingham and Manchester who wanted to supply down here so he told them about this crew, how many, how they dealt and the Manchester lot just saw them off. Someone got hurt, Gloucester people know nothing about real violence, so they backed down and the outsiders came in. It was better that way. They drove down and dealt out of a van in cash or gear up front. Their stuff was better too. I think they had been driven out of their area too. Mind you, they weren't angels either but it wasn't personal."

Penny nodded to encourage her. "So did Jake stay around then?" "Sort of. He had his own girl of course then, several probably knowing him, but he was the one persuaded me into rehab. I was really bad, didn't care where I stuck it or whose needle it was by then. I did a whole year. Social Services said I'd never get Kenny back so I did it to prove to them what I was made of."

Penny pushed a bit further, her mug almost empty now. "So how often have you been seeing Jake recently?" "Oh once a week, twice maybe. If he had some dosh we'd go out for a drink and go back to his place. I've got an old car a friend gave me so I get around now." "And how did Jake get his money then, was he into crime?" Annie looked sideways at her. "I suppose it doesn't matter now does it?" She started to sob a bit.

"He used to pass on information; about anything really. Whose runners were out, how much money they were taking. What places were easy to break into-houses, garages, businesses. Big posh houses, warehouses. If there was any graft anywhere Jake knew about it. Someone who would take a pony and tell you about the alarm system, who could tell you where there were a load of videos being delivered in a van. That's what Jake was good at, knowing people and knowing information."

"So people must have liked him to tell him stuff?" "Oh yeah. He was dead friendly. He knew how to get round people and get them talking; old people, kids, blokes in pubs. He was always on the lookout even when we were down the pub he'd disappear off to the gents and come back with a tenner for something he'd told someone. And he was his own boss. Never got into any gangs-always on the outside-just useful to people."

"And his drug use. Never use any contaminated works?" "No never. That's why he liked me. One in a million; an ex-junkie." "Do you have any idea how he could have died then?" Penny put to her. "I dunno. I tried to call him at the Ram but they said he had not been in for days. He hadn't got a phone. He was run out of Gloucester in the end. Got into a row with some guys whose shop was done over. They thought it was him as he'd done some odd jobs for them. He got the code for the alarm and gave it to someone later."

"Annie, you know the papers have been going on about the plague in Worsley. Well this is what killed Jake. Have you any idea how he would have caught it? Annie was pale with apprehension. "He was the one with plague? That bloke in the papers? I can't believe it." She blinked as her brain worked. "Could I have it then?" she looked terrified now. "I think you would have symptoms by now, it's over a week since he died. I assume you did not see him after he died?"

"Of course not. He didn't like me going to his place unless he said. He used to ring me up and suggest somewhere for a night out. I'd go and collect him in the car and we'd go from there. If he didn't ring it wasn't odd, he just had not earned that week." "When did you last see him then?" "A week before the bank holiday, Saturday. We went for a drink in Worsley, in the Ram, then up the M5 to Tewkesbury, had a meal in the Rat and Parrott. It was really hot and loads of people in there. It's a big club place and it was stuffed with people, head bangers, plenty of deals for Jake too. We went back to his place after about two am I'd guess." "Did you notice anything odd then? Was he sweaty or ill? Any rashes?" "No nothing. It was two am and we were smoking dope mind you. I don't remember much at all. It was a good night." She began to dab at her eyes again recollecting there would not be another night with Jake.

"Did he say he knew anyone who was sick?" "No he was up. Said he'd got a good supply of dosh coming from somewhere. He'd found something or somewhere he reckoned could get him lots of dosh. He did not say where. Could have been an empty house or a van load of stuff from somewhere. It wasn't drugs though. And he seemed to think it would go on, like there'd be more where that came from." "Was that to do with anyone else?" Penny was pressing her. "No, he did say it was his for the taking and no one else knew." She thought back to that night and what Jake had hinted at.

"He said 'as long as the fucking kids don't find it', that's what he said. He meant the kids in Stonefield." "So it was a source of money that was new and near Stonefield?" "I suppose so but he didn't say that. Maybe a big house in Worsley with antiques that was empty or something? A lock-up?"

Penny was touched that this woman who must have come to the attention of the police and certainly social services had no reason or wish to hide anything from them. Maybe that was what Jake liked about her, her transparent honesty. Perhaps you got to an age when lies were not relevant anymore. Annie was a good ten years older than Penny but their bond as women in a tragedy enabled them to talk on the same level. Penny did not think Annie would grieve too much over Jake. A few tears, attend a funeral and she would move on. They were a comfort and a convenience to each other not an item.

After she drove back to the station she reported to Mark Benson who was now in charge of tying up loose ends. Soccos had identified eleven sets of prints in Jake's flat. The only set identified was Rob Vincents. They had some blood stains to work on and a few fibres from an acrylic jumper by the front door but no hairs. Youths wore cropped heads these days only Jake's was long and easily identifiable. There were some longer brown hairs in the bed, guessed to be Annie's. Mark was listing all the thirteen to eighteen year olds on the estate to be investigated and finger printed now. He did not relish trying to persuade their parents, most of whom probably bought and sold stuff to Jake themselves. They'd start at Rob's and try and frighten him into naming others. When he had heard Annie's story, that something big and lucrative was coming Jake's way he was alerted to something one of the other residents had said. "Jake was full of stories-ghosts and zombies who could rise from the dead." Apparently he had only started this nonsense in the last few weeks. Maybe they were connected?

Penny had already gone through Jake's offending records dating back over the years. Drive whilst disqualified three times as a teenager, possess cannabis twice, burglary of a lockup, a shed and some garages in the suburbs of Gloucester over seven years ago. She checked his co-defendants; petty offenders, hardly known now; even Jake had disappeared off their current software. They decided Penny would follow up some enquiries in Little Meadows and anyone who had a view of the path up to the bunker. If Jake had any confidants it was those at the bunker meetings. Maybe they'd know about Jake's new source of wealth.

Rose sat down across the table from Danny and put a plate of half pounder, chips and beans in front of him. She had persuaded him to turn off the TV and sit at table which was unusual for them. "Danny love, you know Jake died of a disease don't you?" she started. He looked at her but said nothing. "They think it's the plague, but I expect its some new virus they haven't found out about before. Did you ever go to his flat?" Danny stuffed a big mouthful of burger and chips in his mouth. "No" he grunted through the food.

"I won't be cross, it's just if there is something catching I need to know if you went there," Danny looked weary like an old man. He finished chewing and took a swig of coke. "No Mum I never went there. They don't let you till you're one of them, grown up you know." "So how did you know him if you didn't go to his flat?" "I didn't know him, not like that." "But you looked really upset when he died."

"He was just different. Everyone said he was great. He was never down, always had plans, ideas. I wish I could be like that." Rose was stunned. "He was a scag head, Danny, an addict. He lived on the dole. Don't you want anything better than that?" Danny gave her a look that said 'if you can't listen don't ask questions'. "I don't know. Don't keep asking me."

"I am sorry. I know the other boys followed him. He must have had something that attracted people to him. Look I'm sorry I never stayed with your Dad. I know how much you would have liked a Dad of your own." Danny and Rose both looked shocked at her saying it out loud.

"It's alright Mum," he said shoving more chips into his mouth. He had spent the last four years wishing he had a dad but he wasn't ready to tell anyone else that, certainly not his mother. He did not want her to think she had failed him in any way. After he swallowed another mouthful he felt he should reassure her.

"We've been alright together haven't we Mum?" he tried. "Yes love, but there are things I can't do that a man can. I thought perhaps Lenny or Mike would have been alright but you never took to them." "They weren't my Dad were they?" "No but blokes know things that women don't think of. You'd learn things off them." "Like what?" Danny looked suspicious. "Well, like about girls how to chat them up, fishing; I don't know, blokes talk about different things."

Danny smiled secretly. So his Mum did know why Jake was important. Jake knew all that. How to get around people, chat them up, make friends, make people like you, get respect. He had not been to his flat but he hung around when the other boys were there at the back of the flats. Danny liked Billy too but was scared of him as well. You never knew when he was going to turn nasty. It was like he had something to protect and just when you thought he was friendly he'd smack you round the head and make fun of you. At school Danny tried to be like Billy but it was not in him. He had two mates, but neither of them were bullies like Billy. He would need to be on Billy's side when he went to school in Gloucester.

Rose went on.

"I wish you had a brother or an uncle you could go out with. I know uncle Raymond's around but he's a bit of a dick head really." Rose's sister's husband was the ideal husband but not much of a role model for Danny. He worked at the post office in Gloucester and rode there by bicycle; in fact he did everything by bike and wore lycra shorts and a crash helmet. He went out on Sundays with his cycling club leaving Melanie with the car which she often used to collect Rose and Danny and take them up to the Cotswolds or go to the river. She had two daughters, one older and one younger than Danny, who were too precious to be any fun at all, but Danny did get to the Wildlife Park, the circus and the waterpark with them. He hated to admit it but it was miles better than hanging around the playground with the other boys at weekends. Uncle Raymond was a spare part anyway. All he talked about was maps, weather and gardening. He did not seem to know anything about cars or music or drugs and Danny wondered how he had got so old while being so stupid and still managed to father two children.

"He's your brother in law Mum, you shouldn't say he's a dick head," Danny laughed. They both laughed and she felt ashamed that the person she felt most affinity with was her own son. Her own flesh. He would be great when he was grown up but now she knew she must not treat him like a mate. "Is your tea OK?" pouring more coke from the giant size bottle. "Will they have a funeral for Jake?" asked Danny out of the blue. "I suppose so. I don't know who his people are. They might bury him somewhere where his family live."

"What about the plague? Does that mean they'll have to burn him?" "I don't know love. Most people get cremated these days anyway. What a creepy conversation." "If he gets a funeral can I go too?" Rose did not want to get into a conflict just now. "You said you hardly knew him. It's supposed to be family at funerals." "I did know him. He used to hang out in the playground at nights. He told great stories about vampires and black magic. He knew all that stuff. He knew everything."

Rose started to wonder if Jake had some other motive than pushing drugs on kids. "What sort of black magic?" she asked warily. "Like putting spells on people. Jake said you didn't need to get into fights you just got a bit of their hair or nails and put it in a jar with some other stuff, said the magic words and something horrible happened to them!" It was Rose's turn to laugh. "I wish that was true! There's a few round here I'd like to do that to. What about the vampires then?" Danny was getting into his stride.

"They've got two big fangs like dogs they bite people with and they can turn into smoke and get into people's rooms under the door or through the keyhole and turn into vampires on the other side. Then they wait until you're asleep and bite your neck and once they've drawn blood you're their slave for life!" "And you believe all that do you?" she gave Danny an old fashioned look. "Well not much but Jake said they really did exist in Europe years ago and they never die neither." Danny finished his chips and licked his lips.

"Any pudding?" "You can have an ice lolly if you like." Rose loved it when they were like this; joking and chatting. Most of the time Danny was out with mates or watching TV or on his Gameboy. Toys made things worse. All the gadgets made it harder and harder for her to talk with him these days.

Chapter Twelve

Lull before the storm

The household was at peace for a short while now Squire Martyn was in Bristow on business. Rebecca, despite being humiliated by Suzannah's position with her husband, still benefitted in the calm and regained a little colour. Rather than her listless self she was almost agitated; ordering the servants and scolding the children and making Suzannah do every little task at her command so that she hardly had time to sit.

"Fetch my new silks from the drawer, and don't twist them about". Suzannah rose and went to the drawer. "You must be more delicate in your ways Suzannah. No other household would put up with such a clumsy girl". Suzannah, whose fingers were fine and white, opened the drawer and carefully picked up several skeins of silk thread. She feasted her eyes on them, golds and reds and greens. She knew the blue silks were so much more expensive as was vermilion. All the dyes came from so many sources in the world. She would love to be able to afford to sit and sit working silks of such quality. Her embroidery had to be wool twine, spun by a village woman and died with local herbs and minerals.

At midday they all ate a simple meal of brawn and brown bread with small beer and a saffron cake then Suzannah took Daniel and Catherine to the fields and woods where they could walk freely and play. In the woods they met Roger the servant gathering kindling and he touched his forelock. No longer did the men tease her or look lasciviously at her. Somehow they knew they could not offend their master and so they must know what her situation was. She was not duped into thinking she had earned their respect. She had earned nothing but shame. As they walked she reflected on her choices in life. A year ago she had been so keen to walk out of her father's house and live in the fine house with its sophisticated ways and luxury possessions. Just seeing Rebecca's pearls and gold, her coral ring, all the way from the South Seas, seemed a dream beyond her scope then. Now she had seen the degradation of such trade in Bristow, the black slaves, the cruelty and callousness of men. What suffering did man endure to get the gold and coral out of the earth and the sea? Who profited by their labour? If the inhabitants of the South Sea Islands were treated like the Africans what had they suffered at the hands of men like Martyn?

She began to see that the prayers and readings father William spoke in the Church were so true; God will provide and we should not seek to glorify ourselves with fine clothes and jewels but work to do good for others and live piously. She felt she had given all her worth for a few trinkets and felt demeaned and sorrowful. She determined on Sunday she would enter the confessional and start to admit her pride and avarice and seek benediction for her sins.

But Suzannah did not have the chance to go to church that week. Later in the evening, while it was still light and the sun was setting in a bright orange sky, the servant came into the parlour to say a cart was approaching the house, pulled by two horses. He went out again and confirmed the occupants and returned immediately to say it was Rebecca's family in great distress.

Rebecca ran to the door to witness Sarah being helped down from a wooden cart with baby Thomas in a basket and Richard, crying and disheveled. Charles was pulling at a box from the back of the cart. Rebecca ran over to them. "Sister, Sister, why are you travelling so? Where is the carriage and where is William who was due to escort you here?"

"Oh Rebecca, can you take us in as we stand? The plague has taken hold in Bristow and is come to Bath. We discovered our postilion was struck down in the stables and did not dare go near so we have run from the house and hired this carter to bring us here. Charles has nothing but his coin and a few jewels and I am as I stand. Oh please help us sister."

Rebecca flinched at the word Plague. She knew that people fleeing from towns were the ones to spread it far and wide and just such a cart might be contaminated. Nevertheless they all looked well if a might bedraggled. It was too late if they were infected and she could not turn her sister out with her baby. Charles was paying the carter with gold, who looked mighty pleased, and Rebecca decided she could not deny her own flesh a sanctuary. They were brought inside.

"But where is William? Is he not with you?"

"William is in Bristow. We sent word for him not to return to collect us from Bath tomorrow; that we had fled. God pray he will come direct from Bristow here".

Rebecca's eyes clouded over with the thought. She had allowed her family from a contaminated household, to come to her home when they could be bringing death with them but she could not say no when she was flesh and blood and loved them so. The tiny child was now released from his basket, so bonny, she could not believe he was diseased; God could not be so cruel. She welcomed them into the parlour to drinks and cakes and ordered the cook to prepare for four more guests for dinner. Yet at the back of her mind she was already considering William's predicament. He was in Bristow where the plague was worse; he was already a day behind them and he consorted with whores in dirty places. Might he already be diseased? She shuddered at the thought of his coming to the Hall, with suppurating sores and fever.

Suddenly the wrath she had suppressed for so long against his maltreatment of her rose up and she had a vision which she would never have dared to allow before, the Hall bolted and barricaded against him, all her loved ones inside and he denied, left to rot outside, alone. It was such a risk. Suppose he returned and was well. How would she survive his fury after he found means to batter his way in? Nevertheless she could plan. Quietly she asked Ann Friend and Suzannah to gather the servants and let them know they would be locking the house this evening against all who came. Those who wished to return to their families in the village may go. She knew that by admitting her brother's family she had put others at risk too. Let them decide for themselves.

Suzannah was entreated to take what servants were left to go gather every container in the house, urns, bowls, jugs, ewers, even the silver they served at dinner, to fill with water from the well. Horse buckets, fire buckets, tankards-all were filled with water immediately. The stable boy was ordered to let all the animals out into the fields, horses and cows alike, and for the pig to be set free in the woods. They had sold most of their sucklings but two left she ordered to be killed and soaked in brine to preserve them. Ann was to go with the maid to the barn and gather all the stored apples, crabs and damsons. The maids had already finished milking the cows and returned to the village and set pans of milk for cream, the butter churn and cheeses were all brought into the pantry. Suzannah carried buckets of apples to the pantry and when space ran out into the bedrooms and laid them about in dark corners, on chests and boxes. There was not enough sugar stored for preserving the fruit but Rebecca ordered the damsons to be stowed nonetheless and put in earthenware containers.

By seven all was done. Rebecca explained to the servants what she meant to do. They could choose to leave or remain besieged for the next few weeks. No water could be used for washing, all was for boiling and drinking and cooking. All soil was to be thrown out from a rear window upstairs into the yard at the back of the house. None would enter or leave from this night. On returning Rebecca prayed for an hour that neither her sister nor her family had brought the plague with them. She remained silent about what she wanted for William. She did not sleep. At every minute she expected to hear the thud of boots on the threshold, an angry husband demanding to be let in. How would she cope-could she refuse? He could go to neighbours until she was sure. Would he kill her when he returned? No sound came in the night. At dawn she called her maid, who had remained, to check Charles and Sarah in their beds. The little ones were sleeping with Suzannah, Catherine now sharing a bed with Maria.

Extraordinarily Rebecca felt she could trust Suzannah more than anyone to stand by her. Both of them were the victims of the same deranged and debauched man and at least she had the respectability of marriage but she recognized Susannah was powerless in his household. A small chink of compassion had crept into her opinion. The great front door was barred in three places and the lock closed. Rebecca had the keys and similarly the yard door, also barred and locked. The windows on the ground floor had their shutters bolted all day and only the upstairs ones were open to the air. The cattle were lowing, waiting to be milked. Rebecca had let the servants who fled home know that they might milk them and do as they wished with the cattle, but the panic over strangers coming from Bath, bringing the plague, kept the locals away from the house.

It was late afternoon when the clopping of hooves was heard coming along the drive to the house, not hastily nor purposely, but meandering and slow. Charles was the first to be aware and Rebecca ran upstairs to an open window to see out. The windows had been covered with muslin and lavender branches to keep out the miasma and she tweaked aside the curtain to look out. Her plan was to tell William that they had already been infected and he was to go to their friends until all were deceased, but she needed not to.

It was clear as the horse came into view that William was very ill indeed. Bubonic plague takes twenty four hours to contaminate and in as short a time to kill. Those less lucky take longer to die, a few survived the fever but by what means no one knew. William slid from his horse outside the front door, then using the handle of his sword, banged on the studded doors. The household froze. Servants dropped their pots and cloths and Charles joined his sister in law at the window.

"He has it. I saw the sores on his face!" Rebecca hissed, "We cannot let him in now."

William started roaring and shouting and looking about the barred windows. He slipped and fell once but managed to stagger up again. Rebecca felt unable to speak and in her eyes he had become nothing, a diseased monster that threatened her children. The monster that had forced his way into her rooms to defile her. Now it was apparent to all that she felt no need to explain to him. The last remaining maid ran to the kitchens in terror and cowered, fearing that he may gain entry. Suzannah stood in the hall struck dumb at the prospect of this disease being on their very doorstep. The butler came behind her and indicated the doorway.

"We cannot refuse to let him in; he is the master, this is his house."

"No Cowle, he is no longer master here, he is corrupted and dying. If you let him past the door we will all die for certain."

Cowle was torn between his duty and his sense. He knew that if the master survived he and all the servants could be executed for failing to protect their master. He imagined the squire coming after them once he recovered and he and his family turned vagabond and exiled. He drew close to the door and Suzannah had to tear at his arm.

"Keep away. Do not let him know you are behind the door it will rile him the more. Only leave him to his fate and he will be dead before long. See how he rails and rants. That is not a sane man".

Cowle gnawed at his knuckles but at least Charles had taken the keys to all the shutters into his care and was prepared to defend them with his sword. Suzannah persuaded him to come back to the kitchens where the squire's ranting was muted.

William began to stagger round the house banging on the windows with his pommel.

"Let me in you she-wolf; this is my property; you cannot deny me entry!" He stumbled on to the back of the house. "I will skin all you servants alive if you do not obey me; let me in now!"

Charles returned downstairs fearing that in their loyalty and conditioning a servant might be coerced into opening a door or window downstairs and he needed to ensure this was prevented. The maids, the footman, and the stable boys had all taken leave the day before, but the cook and the butler were cowering in the buttery that had no windows to the outside. Squire Martyn was now hammering on the back door that was not so sturdy and had a two inch gap beneath it. Rebecca had ordered all the cracks and gaps to be blocked with old linen and rags and William began to tug at the cloths pressed against the back door. His shouting and cursing went on for a half hour then he desisted, presumably exhausted.

He had actually gone to the well, his fever burning him up and he sank the bucket and doused himself in water.

Still in his finery for Bristow, the brocade waistcoat, his best suede coat with the hand painted bone buttons, his frills and lace and at a glance he looked like any wealthy burgher, but on closer inspection he was a demented sight. On his neck a large abscess had formed, black and oozing, staining his lace cravat. His eyes were bloodshot and his gums were bleeding. His breath was rasping and sweat poured down his face. He took the leather bucket and poured it over his head drenching his fine clothes, then with difficulty sent it back down the well for more water. Before pulling it out again he stumbled back to the windows, feebly trying to pull at the wooden shutters and cursing the while.

Eventually his strength was dissipated and with the water ladle in his hand he stumbled towards the meadow where a cow, wanting to be milked, stared glumly back. In his anguish he threw the ladle at the cow and fell face forward into the grass. The cow veered away and cantered off. There was silence.

For the best part of an hour the family and servants had been struck dumb, listening to their master rant and rave, terrified of his curses, but more fearful that he should bring them death. Rebecca, to everyone's surprise, took charge and was the most determined. She had not put up with all her suffering for them to succumb to death now. She checked all the children, ordered more lavender water and drenched cloths with the healing balm. She bade the children cover their mouths with the cloths and put more cloths at the windows and back door. She then assembled all the inhabitants in the hall. The servants needed to be prised out of the pantry, praying and crossing themselves, the butler looked shattered and grey and even Charles was drawn and white with strain. She asked Suzannah to take the children up to Maria's bedroom (that looked out the front of the house), and to play a game to take their minds off the fear in the household.

"My husband is dying of the plague" she solemnly intoned. "He is not himself and is no longer considered to be your master. He is not to be obeyed. He is past this life and any person attempting to help him will be struck down in the same way. The illness will take him shortly and although we do not know what form this takes, whether bad air or contagion or the will of God, for now we will remain inside and let no one near the house, nor let anyone remove". She drew breath; everyone in the room was hanging on her every word.

"We have grain enough to make bread, ale and wine in the buttery and apples and preserved meats. We can live a good while if necessary. No one is to use water for washing. It is to be boiled before using and then kept for brewing and boiling food. In this way God will preserve us. Let us now pray".

All in the room knelt with her. There was no dissent because her assuredness had convinced them their own worries about abandoning their master and not seeking to rescue him were futile, not immoral and against God's will. Suzannah, occupying the children upstairs, was in turmoil. Now separated from her dear family she feared that the plague, which for the moment was contained outside the hall, would reach them and they would soon be dead. On the other hand she knew it was brought with travelers. Both the Gurney family and Sir Martyn had come from the cities bringing death with them. She prayed for forgiveness from

God for her iniquity and that her own family be preserved even if she did not deserve to live.

By dark the family were recovering. Bread was being made in the kitchen with fresh herbs and salt. Smoked joints of pork were sliced up and the remainder of the poultry roasted for dinner with greens that were now cropping this month. The cook was frightened that after a week the poultry would run out and they would be confined to salt pork every day and at every meal. She checked the cheeses; some were from last year and good and hard. There were earthenware pots also with chutneys from crab apples and hawthorn berries so at least she would fashion two types of meals. Oats were in plenty and gruel would be served for breakfast. She prayed that her son and his wife in the village, the blacksmith, would survive the miasma.

Outside William's death was a tormented one. In his fever he did not pray but cursed all the household including "that whore Suzannah" who had bewitched him. Unable to get up, he thrashed about in the long grass of the meadow, sinking into unconciousness by dark and dead by midnight. His foul, stinking body would lie there for a week, before anyone dared to turn their minds to its disposal.

CHAPTER THIRTEEN

QUARANTINE

ROSE WAS WORRIED about the quarantine. It had been on for five days now and no one wanted to leave the village for fear of aggression. A van selling food had come round the estate the third day, cashing in on people's need. Luckily she had got her money from her pub job so had been able to buy a few essentials, bread, milk, potatoes and beans. The frozen stuff in the van was twice the price of Iceland. She would wait until Melanie had the car and brought some stuff back from Gloucester. The police let people hand stuff over. She could pay Melanie when she could cash her books. For now she was raiding the freezer. She guessed other women on the estate would be round soon; she had thought about that. They would know she was the sort of person to have food in store and she did not want to give them stuff which would encourage a liaison not to mention letting them in the house.

There was a young mother on the floor below whose baby was only six weeks old. Social Services had brought out milk powder for her, but little else. Rose had called in a few times, to offer advice or support but the girl only seemed interested in money and Rose had none of that to give away.

After five days of isolation people were beginning to communicate more. Rose had a few friends locally that were not too grubby and whom she could trust to let into her own flat. They sat in her flat on the sixth day discussing the impact of the quarantine.

"Them poor old dears in the bungalows, having to buy off that van at double the price. The Social should be doing something for them, not parasites," her friend Mo grumbled. "I asked my brother to come up from Yate in the car so I could get to Cribbs Causeway and he refused. He thought he'd get the plague!" said Sharon.

"Do you think it will go on much longer?" Mo made a roll up. No one else has been sick. They've been in every flat on this estate with their masks and plastic suits, swabbing this, swabbing that. No one tells us anything and we're most at risk." "How can someone get the plague these days anyway," moaned Sharon, "That's like Medieval. No one has the plague now."

Rose felt perplexed. Sharon was right. There was no explanation. So Jake went out in a car sometimes; Birmingham or Bristow. He had not been abroad. Maybe he had caught it off some immigrant he had met. She could not believe there were vampire bats in the Cotswolds, someone would have said.

"I've had my kids home all week," said Mo. "It's just hell. Mikey's started tearing the wallpaper off he's so bored and the kid is getting bullied by him. Can't they open the youth club in the day and give them something to do?" It was a good idea but Mo was not going to ask anyone in authority. And who would come? The youth club was closed till further notice. The neighbours were in and out of each other's homes, the queue for the food van bringing people together. Everyone gleaned a little more information from a health worker or an environment officer. All the tales got embellished. After a week the rumours were that Jake had been dealing with the Triads in Birmingham, that a swarm of vampire bats had set up home in Worsley woods and were coming out at night and biting people; everyone knew Jake left a window open at night. Neighbours were saying that injecting heroin gave you bubonic plague and that Jake was head of a coven of witches who sucked blood and had zombies at their command.

After a week the all clear was given on the flats and everyone in the area had been tested and found negative. Jake turned out to have a mother living near Monmouth who arranged for a memorial to take place but no one in Worsley was invited. Somehow Penny Worstham got through to her and let her know about Annie who was invited to Gloucester Crematorium although once there she found she was unable to cry at all. Twenty years of friendship and not a tear shed.

Once the body was disposed of and no one had any more symptoms the story lost its interest in the public arena. The reporters went away, the flats were condemned as uninhabitable, the buses started running again. There was not much else to say about it in the estate and people stopped mixing with their neighbours. Rose felt obliged to keep up the contact with the girl downstairs; somehow she had bonded with the tiny baby and Shelley, the mother, was grateful to go out one or two nights a week.

This signalled a change in Danny's life. Rose was bringing the baby up to the flat; changing nappies, getting bottles warmed up. Danny could see his mother was pre-occupied with baby things and felt left out. He hated babies; smelly, dirty and sickly and cried all the time. Even his second-hand playstation did not keep him in. It was only another four weeks to the end of term, hardly worth going back to school, thought Danny.

The school bus started turning up again on the Monday and hardly any kids got on it the first day. They had had half term then a week off, easy to play on the local drama. By the time the welfare officer got there it would be July and too late to go back anyway. The kids had got used to hanging around all day; the nights were warm though and parents were traipsing round the flats looking for errant children at midnight. No one seemed to know where any of them got to anymore.

Danny felt more and more isolated. He had always had his Mum to himself. He could be truculent and rude sometimes to Rose but underneath he would never have upset her. But now, with this baby, it was like he was not there anymore. She had even forgotten to make his tea yesterday and she had been in all day. Danny wanted more and more to find some father figure; someone who would notice him. He wanted to be important to someone, to be different, to be appreciated. He spent every night hanging around the derelict playground with the others listening to stories about what girls did, what they were like, what you could do to them. What drugs did to you, what it was like, how it felt. He got some of the rough cider inside him and shared roll ups with older boys. He just felt too young. He was eleven in September but felt like a teenager. Every day in the mirror he checked out his body for signs of puberty, the odd stray hair but nothing very manly appeared anywhere. He looked at mucky books but nothing happened if he got a stiffy. He could not wait to grow up.

One evening he overheard Billy and one or two others planning to go up to Marj McCormacks; he made to follow but Billy scorned him in front of the others. "You can't come, it's for blokes not little kids" Billy hissed. Danny made up his mind he was going to see some of the action even if he was not allowed in. He had seen some amazing pictures in magazines; women with tits like balloons, their legs wide open showing everything. What if Marj did things like that? He knew from Stonefield you could scale up the balcony to the first floor. Marj lived on Cornfield, but what would be the point if she had the curtains closed? He just wanted to know what Billy and his friends did to her.

He waited twenty minutes then went to the outside of Marj's flat and looked up at the balcony. It was hardly dark at nine thirty but he could see lights on behind the net curtains. Would it be worth it? What would happen if he got caught? Was being a peeping tom a crime? Who would report him if it was? He looked around him. People from Stonefield could see if they chose, it was about three hundred yards to the nearest block. No one was outside on this side tonight. He scanned the walls below the balcony looking for toe holds. There was some old wiring and metal fastenings he could get his foot to and he was tall but light in build. By using a bit of metal sticking out he could just reach a bit of electric cable half way up the wall. If that held he could reach up to the balcony. He did it. One minute he was on the ground, the next he had hooked his leg over the balcony rail. His soft trainers made no noise and the window at the side of the balcony looked into a bathroom. No one in there. He could hear laughter and music from the living room beyond. Boy's voices and Marj getting drunk. He could not hear what they were saying but guessed they were encouraging Marj as she was whooping and laughing as they egged her on. Suddenly the light next to the balcony came on and by leaning out Danny could see through a chink in the curtain Marj standing on the bed. She appeared to be staggering on top of the mattress holding up her nightdress. Danny could hear Billy's voice and one other goading and cheering and saw the other boy come round to the window side of the bed, dropping his trousers as he went. Danny was mesmerised. The slim boyish figure had his back to Danny but was clearly ready for action. Danny saw Marj slip or sink on to the bed and the boy got in beside her. Billy was on the other side of the bed and Danny watched the whole time. Two boys at once! He wished he was one of them.

Billy was getting bored with Marj. She had shown him a thing or two; there were no holds barred with her but he wanted to impress a real girl, a virgin if possible. He had been watching the girl with the pink mouth before they were banned from school and now all he could think of was what he could do with that mouth. Not old Marj's flabby mouth, he wanted taut, he wanted fresh, he wanted slender. He determined that whatever the others said he would be on that school bus tomorrow and he would have something to impress the girl with as well.

Danny went home feeling distinctly frustrated. He was in a bad place. Too old for kid stuff and too young to join in with adult pursuits. He was sick of Rose cuddling that baby and just wanted to get somewhere on his own. He wandered up to the bunker most nights just for something to do. Now Jake was dead the door was locked up and no one went there. Nick and Eddy were old enough to get a moped and ride about now, if illegally, and Nick used his to go up to the Ram to see if anyone was selling dope. The £50 worth off Jake had lasted the week but now they had run out. The Ram was beginning to fill up again now a week had passed and on the Monday the environmental health had issued a statement to say there was no further quarantine around Worsley. Ron's cousin came over and offered Nick a deal but it was exorbitant. Apart from going to Gloucester who else was going to bring stuff in? Despite wanting £30 for an eighth Ron's cousin was amazed to see Nick produce the money without demur. They had shared out the £130 four ways but the eighth would have to do all four of them tonight. Without the bunker they were forced to sit outside, backs against the garages, the evening hot and dry.

"So why can't we break into the bunker again?" said Billy. "No one's been up here to check it have they?" "How can we get through a steel door with a padlock?" added Nick. "My neighbour's got bolt cutters that can get through any padlock," said Billy, "but I can't get them off him without him asking questions." "I bet Ron's got bolt cutters," said Nick. It's OK now in June but come October we don't want to be freezing our butts off for a smoke."

Initially no one liked to talk about Jake but by a week they had begun discussing some of his theories. He had said people rose from the dead and he knew spells on how to contact them. Where did he get to know this they wondered;

he never went out far. Where did he meet all these satanic people? Was Annie a witch they wondered? As none of them knew anything for real they were left with a muddled fantasy about zombies and witchcraft that had somehow ended in Jake's death. They did not want to go there; they wanted their old life back in the bunker where they felt safe.

On Monday 14th June the school bus turned up at 8 am as it had done two weeks ago. Billy was waiting. In uniform with a clean shirt he had persuaded his mother to iron. Even his mother was stunned. She had always had to goad and shout to get him up before. Billy had been thinking a lot about the girl and he had formed a plan. He would take some money with him and try chatting her up so see if she would go with him for a drink. He didn't reckon they could get into a pub but there was a cafe in town that was cool and played good music. He could invite her there now he had all the money he needed.

He hung out in the playground at lunch time on his own and spied her coming out of the girls toilets. She disappeared round the back of the gym; he knew she was going for a fag so he followed her. She was with two mates but Billy had been practicing what to say and do. He chatted them all up. In fact by being more attentive to one of her mates he could see out of the corner of his eye that she was looking. First he talked about what he did after school then got round to asking them what they did. They did in fact hang around in Gloucester before getting the bus home, chatting up boys. Tanya, as she was, agreed to go into Gloucester with him at 4pm.

Billy came away ecstatic. Fifteen and his first chat up successful. He just had to play it cool and in his pocket he fingered his piece de resistance, Jake's blue and pearl ring. He could not wait for four o'clock and two hours seemed interminable but eventually the teacher said go and he tried to saunter casually to the school lockers in a nonchalant manner, his heart beating. They arranged to meet outside the school gates and he was disconcerted to find her two friends were coming too. As they were all going into town he decided it was OK and practiced his favourite one-liners on them as they walked and they obligingly giggled at the right times. As they walked into Gloucester they lit up and Billy let it be known he had dope on him.

Tanya and her friends were in the same class but she looked younger than them and seemed disconcerted by his worldliness. He decided he had better play it cooler and started discussing music with her and sharing their favourites as they gradually dropped behind her two friends. He could not take his eyes off that perfect peach-coloured cupid's bow of a mouth. She had long reddish hair, straight and shiny. Her eyes were not spectacular, a sort of hazel more than green, but her skin was so fine he could see through it. Her body was slim and straight with long limbs and a tiny straight skirt hardly half way down her thighs. Somehow he knew she was not experienced sexually so in that way he had the upper hand. She seemed apprehensive and demure but nevertheless seemed keen to be with him. He had hoped for a bit more banter but maybe she was just nervous.

Eventually they got to the café and bought cakes and milkshakes. He started telling her about life in Worsley. Put in to words it sounded a bit dull so he decided to spice it up a bit. "Me mates and me belong to this secret group. We meet up at night in our own secret room. Its blokes only; girls'd be too scared to go there at night".

"What do you do there?" she looked curious and not shocked. "Oh we discuss things like vampires and black magic and zombies, and swap knowledge," he added although that was not true now Jake was dead. She started to look uncomfortable. "So how do you get zombies?" "Well it's like vampires, you have to get bitten by one". Billy realized his knowledge was actually quite limited. "But I can't really talk about it," he havered. "And that's what you talk about?" Billy realized how daft he was sounding. "Oh lots of things; ghosts, whether people come back from the dead." Her two friends sitting a table away were beginning to giggle.

"Who else is in this secret club then?" Billy could see a way to impress her. "Well, you know that bloke who died? He was one of us". He waited for the gasp of admiration but Tanya looked even more sceptical. "He was some old bloke-a junkie wasn't he?"

"Yeah but now he's gone they'll need a new leader now," said Billy. She was losing interest. "So what does the leader do then?" Billy was stuck now as he was hardly qualified to do what Jake did. "Just when we meet up, say who is allowed to join and supplies the puff." She was still unnerved. "So you are really into drugs then." He was trying to work out which way to jump. "Nah, I can take it or leave it." he tried. "I think it turns your brain funny," she replied. Billy felt he was losing the game a bit as she started to look at her watch. "I'm just going to phone my Mum."

She proceeded to speak to her mother saying she would be home by 5pm. Billy felt desperate to keep her interest. As she put the phone down he produced the ring from his pocket. "This is the leaders ring. He gave it to me before he died and said "You take over from me Bill. If anything happens to me." "So he knew when he was going to die then?" Now Billy wondered if she was taking the mick. "I guess he had an aura or something," he said trying to remember the right words. "He definitely knew about all sorts of weird stuff, history and that, sci-fi, aliens, that sort of thing." Billy held up the ring in the light which shimmered on the pearls. Tanya did sit up then. "Billy, that's beautiful." He held it up in his right hand and pushed it over his middle finger on his left hand. As he did so he felt a sharp stab on the side of his finger but tried not to wince. Two people at the next table were looking now so he put his hand down. The ring looked too big on his hand but made him feel powerful. He had never seen it on Jake's hand when they were in the bunker. He must have started wearing it in the last week before he died.

Suddenly she was getting up. "I'd better get my bus now. Thanks for the shake."

"Can we see each other again?" he tried. He was beginning to think he had overdone the supernatural bit. It was only to get her excited. "Yeah, we could come here tomorrow. I'll swap you the CDs I've got OK?"

Now he knew he was in with a chance. Even the long trip home on the public bus was worth it to see her again. He dithered about trying to kiss her but left it too late. "Maybe we could go to see a film this week. Like Friday?" She laughed for the first time. "Nightmare on Elm Street is on. That sounds like your sort of movie!" She waved goodbye and strode off. Billy took off the ring and put it back in his pocket. He didn't want some beat copper asking where he got it. He didn't know where Jake got it, it must be stolen. Probably on some police list; it was very old-looking. On the bus home he tried to recall what Jake had said. Something about where there was plenty more, he wouldn't have to work anymore, he seemed pretty confident too. On top of the bus as people got off he took it out again to look examine it better. He noticed he had a slight scratch on his finger and saw inside the ring there protruded a sliver of silver. He tried to push it back without success. "I must fix that tonight so I can wear it properly," he thought. He sat and day-dreamed out of the window until the bus pulled into Meadows Drive. It was a brilliant day, the sky as blue as the sea and the horizon showing a green line where the sun was slipping westward and a balmy breeze blew across the estate. Billy wanted to dance up the street singing and telling everyone he'd got a girl of his own; no more visits to Marj for him.

Billy got indoors but his mother was watching Gladiators and hardly looked round. "Tea's in the oven" she said over her shoulder. Billy looked in. Mum's beef pie, peas and chips. He went into his room, took off his school clothes and put on tracky bottoms and a T shirt. He got his dinner and a tea towel and sat down in front of the TV. His finger was itching now and he sucked it, then tucked into his meal. "Thanks Mum." His mother looked at him astounded. He never said thanks, he never went to school on time. He was usually grumpy. "Have you had a good day then?" she tried. "Yeah OK. He could hardly suppress his smile. "School's school." "Anything special happen today?" "No same old lessons and Mr Jarrett kicked me out of geography again. French teachers off sick. That's three weeks. Everyone wanted to know about the plague of course."

"People are just ghoulish; we've been tarnished by that Jake dying like that. No one will want to know anyone from Worsley now. The towns name will be famous as as the Worsley Plague, like they said in the papers." "Don't be daft, Mum. It'll be forgotten in a week. Even people here are more interested in footie and who is screwing who," His mother grimaced. "I don't care, I don't like it. Why did we have to end up here?" "Billy was getting fed up with this. "Because you never paid the rent in our last place, wasn't it." "You don't know what it's like trying to keep up with the bills on time. You don't bring anything in. Why don't you get a job this summer? A paper round or something." Billy was going to reply in his usual manner but thought twice. "I was thinking today I might like to join the police one day." His mother gasped. "You never stop cursing them, Billy. What changed your mind?" "I was thinking how they get good pay and can break the speed limit when they like. And they break the law and get away with it."

She laughed. Maybe things were going to be alright after all. Billy finished his dinner. "That was ace Mum." She took his plate. "Are you going out?" He stretched out on the sofa. Life was the best now. "Yeah but not now though. I want to catch Eastenders."

Billy's mother had had a job in Gloucester; only part time. They had told her she would be better off but she wasn't. She'd lost half the perks of Social Security and got less money and she had lost track of the paperwork till the rent arrears were so high she had been evicted. Once in Worsley there was no chance of a job as the travel costs were so high. She had a bit of home work, stuffing envelopes. And there were no blokes there worth meeting. She had had a vague idea that once Billy was off she could move back to town and get a private bedsit and support herself. If she could meet a decent bloke in Gloucester he may look after her. Roy had money but he was weak and Billy could run rings round him already. And he was married and was not going to leave his wife.

"They sat in silence as they watched TV. Billy got up and made some tea and gave his mother a cup. Again she looked surprised but said nothing. "You seeing Roy tonight?" he queried. "No he's coming Wednesday for tea. Will you be in?" "Not if you don't want me to be. I'm going to the movie on Friday though." "So you want some money then?" Billy realized that if he said no she would want to know where he was getting it from so he said nothing. Roy could afford it anyway if he wanted to come back Friday evening. Eventually he got up, ran some water through his hair and gelled it, cleaned his teeth and washed his hands. His finger was still itchy but there was no sign of bleeding. He took the ring out of his trouser pocket and put it back in the bed frame and took out twenty pounds. He didn't want to see Marj but he was gasping for a drink and Monday was the day her mate brought the cider over.

He strolled out across the can-littered space between Little Meadows and Stonefield. Never had Stonefield seemed such a pleasant place to live. Everyone he saw he knew and everyone he knew liked him, as far as he knew. He had a slight pang that Jake would not be there anymore; no one to organize the drugs or tell stories or get people doing things, but he was a bit of a creep. Why did he only have friends who were kids? What was all that stuff about zombies? It was rubbish really. When he saw how Tanya responded he realised he was being a kid believing all that twaddle. Maybe he could have a better secret group, crime, weapons, drugs and booze, if they could get the door off the bunker again. He kept turning it over in his mind; who would be in charge, could he run it? Eddy and Nick were really too old for secret gangs but he was just the right age to coerce some thirteen year olds into the club. That Danny was good enough, pity he was only eleven. They would still need to prove themselves like before. Maybe Danny could steal something from one of the big houses. He was small enough to get through a toilet window. Billy hung around the playground for a short while then went to Marj's for a load of cider, He was back indoors by 10 o'clock and went to bed happy.

Alice Best was back at the Burn's flat that night. Frankie was as agitated but less preoccupied with zombies and more obsessed with the plague. She was now convinced all of Worsley was on the verge of a epidemic. She did not leave her flat except to get her methadone and a few personal items from the chemist. Her mother, whilst still unconcerned, was getting exasperated having to do everything at home for her. "You'd never think she was seventeen. Never cooks, washes her sheets, nothing. I get no help at all and she never goes out now." Alice felt helpless. "Maybe she should be referred to a psychiatrist for assessment. Sometimes drugs can make people mentally ill." Frankie's mother looked aggrieved. "Anything to get her out of the house for a day. She gets on my wick."

"Has she got any friends who don't use drugs." Asked Alice seriously. "Who would want to be friends with her?" All this was said in front of Frankie who seemed oblivious to the insults because she was so preoccupied with her own thoughts. Alice tried again. "Frankie, will you go and see your GP again and let me go with you?"

"Can he give me something to stop me getting the plague?" "I want you to see a psychiatrist to get your head sorted out. He might give you something to relax." Alice observed the girl. She was losing weight and her hair was like greasy string and if she stayed here much longer she would be self-harming or suicidal. Alice decided she would have to badger the doctor into letting her speak to him for the girl's safety. True she was now an adult but mentally she was not capable of making decisions.

When Alice got back to the drugs Centre she found Colin and took him to one side.

"There's something really weird going on on that estate. We know there's lots of drugs about but no one is exhibiting symptoms now they have cleared the flats out. Frankie Burns is going off her head. I don't know why her GP is not taking up the case. She is quite obviously experiencing post traumatic stress disorder. I'm going to have to write a letter. She'll be back on heroin or self-harming if I don't take some action. Colin looked thoughtful. "You don't know what she was like before; maybe she was always paranoid." "All the more reason for an assessment. I can't leave it. I wonder if she knows things she won't tell because it's too awful to admit. Like if she shared needles with Freeman she could be infected with what he had. We don't know how long he was incubating before he died."

Colin shuddered. "He did not appear to be injecting but who knows? It's been four weeks since the first one died and about two weeks since Freeman died. If anyone else was going to be infected we'd have found another one. There are no other injectors on the estate that we know about, but there could be lots we don't know about." Colin was trying to think it through as he spoke but Alice was focusing on the problem they did know about. "I am going to write to her GP. They must respond now there is a notifiable illness about."

In the mortuary Charles Hargreaves and David Champion were inspecting a recent corpse from Gloucester. The body had been found in a decomposed state in a council flat by environmental health officers after the neighbours complained. David introduced the case, "There's no indication of abcesses in the groin or armpits, although it's hard to tell with all that adipocea formed. No maggots either. By my estimate died about two weeks ago. This hot weather has exacerbated decomposition."

Charles removed his face mask. "Not the plague then. We had better take all precautions though. This one must have died the same time as the second victim. Neighbours told the police they had seen him out in his slippers a couple of weeks ago but not since. No one went in to see him apparently." David stepped back. "Preliminary guess I'd say his heart went, he's eighty seven; not surprising really."

Charles left his assistant to prepare the body for post mortem and took a break for coffee in his office. David followed him in. "Have you come up with any explanation for this?" he indicated the Freeman file. David had been doing some research in the library looking up any references to "strange deaths". The last cases of bubonic plague were in Southern China in the nineteenth century. Since then all victims have been bitten by animals carrying the bacteria, squirrels, bats and rats. "It has to be bodily fluids into the bloodstream. That means rough or anal intercourse, bites, intravenous injections, or scratches from infected animals or flea or bed bug bites. We haven't seen a case of bed bugs here for years and no wild animals have been reported to carry plague in Britain. That leaves either human to human contagion or one of these people went to the Americas and got bitten in the last fortnight. We know that is not true of our two cases. Both were drug users, one an injector. We can assume one caught it off the other. So where did the first one catch it from?" Charles started up. "Look I am sure the symptoms of the first body were quite different. Sure there were infected sites but not in the armpits or groin. It was quite different. I think we are looking at a totally single case here. We need to let the police know there were not necessarily any connections between the two to lessen the job of investigating."

Charles Hargreaves sipped his coffee. "In the nineteenth century, when they were digging the London Underground they found numerous plague pits all over London. There's no record of any direct link but the navvies were so reluctant to work near them they did a diversion. That is why Baker Street Line suddenly dips down fifteen feet at one point. It went underneath the plague pits to avoid disturbing them."

David eyed him suspiciously. "But we are talking three hundred years ago or more. Bodies would have disintegrated long before that; especially if they weren't even in coffins."

"True but they initially used lime to kill the infection and lime burns but prevents decay." The two men looked silently at each other. "Is it possible there's something like that here? In a rural area? Surely they'd have no use for plague pits in a village?" "Who knows? In some places the disease just took people by surprise as they stood or slept in twenty four hours. If the whole village died who was left to bury the last few?" Charles started to write notes in his notebook. "We need a local historian and archeologist especially in the Worsley area. See if there is any record of what happened in the villages when the Plague hit." David Champion was already on the phone to the archeology department.

Chapter Fourteen

Damnation

THE HOUSEHOLD HELD its breath overnight and the next dawn Rebecca peered out of the upstairs window to see Williams body lying unmoving in the grass. She and Charles sat in conference in the parlour while Suzannah and Ann Friend tried to amuse five children and explain away the extraordinary behaviour of the adults and the veto on going out of the house. It was an eerie time. No spinette or recorder were heard. The younger ones laughed and played not knowing that their father lay dead outside, nor understanding the seriousness of the situation, only aggrieved that although the sun shone they could not go out into the field. A journeyman came up the drive one day and before he would go to the rear door Ann saw him and waved him away; she did not say we have plague here, but said the village was at risk of infection and he should go the way he came. In this way he would not tell the village what he had seen and spread the news of their shame.

There was no sign of William's horse. Charles and Rebecca agreed they should stay put for a week at least. There was no way of communicating with anyone else without putting either themselves or others at risk. The servants who had left for the village would have spoken of the situation of the fleers from Bath and fear of contamination so no one would come from there until they were sure that either the family had died or had survived. Fortunately the plague ravaged quickly so they would know soon enough of any survivors.

They waited. The servants occupied themselves with food preparation and cleaning and thrice daily prayer book reading in the hall with Rebecca. In between they played knuckle stones and drafts and Charles read to them from the bible. Every day all persons were checked to ensure they had no lesions or fever and all seemed well. The horror that lay not thirty yards from their back door instilled in them a terror that somehow the disease could be creeping across the grass towards them, creeping under the door or through the shutters, waiting to infect them. The water ran low. Cook had brewed three lots of ale in a week but it was all they had to drink and it went quickly. Four servants, three adults and five children were surviving on a dwindling supply of salt pork, small beer and fruit. By the second week cook approached Rebecca.

"We have plenty of pork and bread but the butter is almost gone as is the cheese and the water will not make another batch of ale. By tomorrow we must go to the well".

Rebecca was angry. She had only an hour or two to think and although they had taken as much water as they could the number in the household was too many to make it last. She was pondering whether or not to approach the well, where her husband had used the bucket, would be the death of them. He had used the bucket, he had touched the well handle and the ladle; was the water contaminated?

On the other side of the lane to the drive was a gravelly stream, quite pure but shallow. Trout swam there and she had drunk from there herself in times past. She consulted Charles to see what he would think. An educated and worldly man, he had some knowledge to impart.

"We know nothing of this disease, except that where it breaks out it contaminates everything around it. I do not doubt the well is now poisoned and we cannot risk using it. Men of learning say that it spreads where others are close confined, the poor and on ships. They do not know whether it is the proximity of bodies or the air they breathe, but certainly it is widespread in towns and cities where it spreads from house to house and street to street. We, who were well housed and clean at home were not affected although our stable boy was. Here where there are no other neighbouring houses nor any venturing to the stream its use would not appear such a risk. I will go if necessary."

Charles looked anxious. In his mind he wondered if William had drunk also at the stream, but the water flowed on and had done so for a week now. Surely a sickness could not persevere in wood and grass and water.

"There is another thing" he hesitated. "William's body is attracting flies. They cluster around the meadow where his corpse is. The flies might carry the disease and could easily get into the house. We cannot keep cloths over the windows forever."

Charles called the butler. It seemed unfair to burden the staff with this task but the man could also see the dilemma. Together they devised a plan. They would dig a hole in the meadow for a grave far enough from the body to avoid the flies. They would shroud themselves in sheets soaked in lavender and bay water and with masked faces they could work long enough to dig a few feet down in one day. Then using pitchforks they could roll the body into the hole from as far away as possible. The butler blanched but Charles pointed out that it was Rebecca's foresight that had prevented the master entering the house bringing death to them all. Eventually they agreed that after collecting water from the stream they should undertake the task. Wrapped in sodden linen cloths they had to enter the stables to get pitchforks and shovels but after three hours, unfortunately in the sunlight, they had gone down four feet. Neither had been able to avoid the sight of the body, now crawling with maggots.

It was an incongruous sight, the expensive brocades and leather, the gold and the pearls all mingled with putrefaction. With long hayforks they disturbed the myriad flies but managed to push the body into the hole by rolling it across the grass. Rats had begun to attack the extremities and the smell made them retch. Eventually they were able to toss in the soil and cover the last remains of Squire Martyn. Charles was even able to say a prayer over the grave before they returned to the house. There was a dilemma for all, that now possibly Charles and the butler were, so they decided that for twenty four hours they should remain alone together in the parlour while the rest of the household stayed upstairs. The hours dragged by. Thomas missed his father and cried. Charles and the man drank wine and played drafts and chess to while away the night and day and Charles had, unbeknown to his family a pistol at hand should he feel the effects of the disease come upon him.

Suddenly a rap came at the door. They all stopped what they were doing and turned to Rebecca. She went to the window above the front door to see Suzannah's father Isaac, standing below the window.

"Mistress Martyn, I cannot stay away longer. I must know how my Suzannah is. We heard in the village that you were shutting up the house for fear of the plague. I need to know that my girl is safe and well."

"Fear not Master Garrod, your daughter is safe and healthy here within. Come Suzannah and show yourself to your father." Suzannah rushed to the window and drew aside the muslin. "Oh father I am so pleased to see you. We are all saved by God's grace but how is the family. Are you all safe also?"

"The whole family is well, but why are you still confined?" Rebecca pulled Suzannah away. "It is a precaution Master Garrod. My family joined us from Bath where plague is rife. We closet ourselves to ensure we are not contaminating others. It is only a few days to be sure. Is the village safe?"

Isaac was a little perplexed at having to crane his neck back so stepped aside the better to see Rebecca who still only peeped through the curtains.

"There is no plague here Ma'am. All the villagers are safe and well. Perhaps Suzannah should come back to us for the time being?" Rebecca quickly checked herself. She could not risk Suzannah telling the whole community that William had been buried without a priest. "I need her here. She has been invaluable with the children."

Isaac looked disappointed. "And Squire Martyn? Is he also well?" Rebecca did not hesitate. "We have not seen him;

he remains in Bristow. I fear for his safety but perhaps by staying away he fears for us too."

Charles and Suzannah stared at each other. Rebecca had lied, without hesitation. She had denied her own husband. With this statement she had also incriminated the whole household in the lie.

"He was due back last Friday with my family but they came on ahead a day early". Isaac doffed his cap and went on his way. Assured that his daughter had not succumbed to the plague his errand was completed.

Rebecca returned to their company and stared hard at Suzannah. "As far as all here are concerned my husband never returned. I do not want everyone knowing he was buried here unshriven, putrid and in secret. As far as the village and the church is concerned he died in Bristow and now lies unnamed in a common grave somewhere. No one needs to know the truth."

Suzannah reflected on the value of this untruth. Did she really need to tell her family that Squire Martyn returned festering and dying? Did the servants want to admit they had illegally buried their master? It would be in everyone's interests to forget he ever came here at all. Charles spoke to the servants. He respected them but reminded them they would be in trouble if the law found they had buried someone without disclosure. Best to say he was missing. When the horse was found they would investigate and search between here and Yate but no one would find his body. Suzannah also had a vested interest in keeping silent. If she kept Rebecca's secret then Rebecca must keep hers. She was convinced that Rebecca had known that William was tupping the pretty companion early on and Rebecca could not risk betraying Suzannah for it all to come out in full.

After another three days Rebecca, Charles and Sarah had a conference and decided to open up the house. They had gathered water from the stream, not the well and they still felt afraid the well was contaminated. All the hay and straw around the cart rooms and yard were burned and the stables scrubbed and rid of rats and mice. The cows were rounded up and brought home and the maids came from the village to milk them again.

They had agreed that the Gurney family would remain at Worsley Hall for the foreseeable future as their fear of going back to their house in Bath overcame any concerns about income and business. Charles could send messengers to Bath once they had word the plague had passed to enquire whether it was safe to return and would have to run his business by proxy for the while. Without Squire Martyn Rebecca would need to meet with their lawyer to arrange funds from his bank but for the present there would be no query to that as she had done so on the occasions he had travelled to the Indies and the protocols were all in place. She also knew he had drawn up a will in the case of his death at sea and that whatever he had determined then, some three years ago, was unlikely to have changed. Rebecca felt that she would assume the role of head of the household in his absence and that with Charles and Sarah by her side she would be able to manage the farms at least and Charles could advise her about William's business until he was declared dead.

Rebecca commissioned a new well. She gave no explanation and as she paid handsomely no one queried her request. The old well was filled in in due course, not too soon as she feared people would say her husband was at the bottom of it. The part of the field where her husband was buried was quietly fenced off and an orchard planted there. Charles oversaw the planting as only he and the butler knew the whereabouts of the grave. There was no doubt that the servants, like Rebecca, felt relieved they no longer had to endure the abuse and ire of their master and no one mourned his going.

Chapter Fifteen

The ring

BILLY WAS UP and out at the school bus on Tuesday by eight am. He was smiling and chattering to the other students as they waited for the bus. He had still got a sore finger and decided to leave his ring behind in the bed post today. He would fix the scratchy bit of silver when he had time and could find Roy's toolbox from the car. He met Tanya at break for a fag behind the gym and this time she left her two mates behind. He wanted to ensure they were going to see the film, preferably tomorrow when Roy would give him some money to disappear for the evening.

"So could you go to the flicks tomorrow? he tried. "Nightmare doesn't start till Thursday, don't you want to wait till then?" she asked. "Anyway it's a school day. I've got maths homework and my Dad makes me do it." Billy was curious about people who have Dads still at home. "What's he do then?"

"Sells air-conditioning. Its right boring. That's why he wants me to go to college after school. I just want to be an air-hostess. You get loads of perks as well as travelling everywhere. When I'm eighteen I am going to apply straight away. Billy was a bit taken aback. She was gorgeous to look at, everyone would want her. Why would she be interested in him? "I'd like to be a pilot, me" he said coolly, "I'd be good at driving a plane." She checked herself. "What qualifications do you need for that?" she asked.

Billy was stuck. He had no idea. He had never thought of having qualifications before. Maybe getting work in a pub or making blue movies was all he had thought about before. "Maths. You have to be good at maths" he said confidently. "Well lets meet up at the café again then. I've got money, you can have an ice-cream if you like."

"Oh no, got to look after my figure! But I'll see you outside school at four o'clock."

Billy had never been so excited. The idea of all the other boys seeing him meeting up with Tanya in public and going out with her made him feel high as a kite. He had had a joint at lunchtime to calm down. He felt hot and light headed like he had a fever. He had heard people talk about being lovesick but this was way more than he expected.

At three thirty he was in science. He tried to take notes this time as he may need science to be a pilot. He felt a bit sick and wondered if it was the blow. It had never affected him like that before. By four pm he was sweating and felt hot and cold at once. He sneezed. "Don't say I am getting a cold." He had not had a cold for years as far as he could remember. Tanya was waiting for him. She did not wear makeup but there was something immaculate about her face. He wondered if it was very subtle makeup. They strolled into town towards the café and Billy had already loosened his tie but still felt stifled. It was sunny but not particularly hot for July.

"What's the matter you look all sweaty." Tanya said. "I know, I think I am getting a cold." He had also noticed the cut on his finger had got all infected as well. It was red all the way round now and getting pussy. He hid his hand as he paid for the drinks and kept it under the table as they talked. He found it hard to concentrate on what she was saying. Some stupid story about one of her friends getting raped by a sixth former. Some other students came in. She spent as much time talking to her friends and started laughing and joking between them all. Billy wished they would all go away. In fact he wanted to go away. Go away and lie down. "Billy you look really ill," Tanya remarked as the others left. "You should go home and get some Lemsip or something."

Billy got on the Worsley bus at Gloucester and sat with his head against the window pane leaving a sweaty mark. He did not notice people looking at him. Rose Collins was watching. She thought he looked sick. When they got off the bus Billy stumbled but she did not go near him. She would tell Danny to keep away from him. Billy went home and his mother did not even look as he came in. "Mum, got a cold and I'm going to bed." She was watching Neighbours but after made a cup of tea and took one in for Billy. He did look bad she thought. "Come on, get your school clothes off at least," she chided. Billy sat up dizzily and pulled off his shoes but he did feel really feverish now. His mother took his blazer and tie and then it struck her. "This could be more than a cold," she thought. "He was alright this morning". She went out to the phone box straight away and dialed 999. "Ambulance" she croaked into the phone. "I think my boy's got the plague."

The lights stayed on all night and the ghostly white curtains of the quarantine room gave Evie the creeps. She had to wear a white gown and mask even outside the room but at least she could see Billy all hooked up with tubes. The doctors said it was only because of her quick thinking he even stood a chance and that was 50 – 50. They had all rushed to the hospital in the ambulance and although the paramedics had face masks they were all injected with something. Evie was most at risk and they came and took her vital signs but she felt fine.

They kept asking her questions she could not answer. Who had Billy been hanging around with? Did he use drugs? Where did he cut his finger? She knew he smoked but they found some resin in his pocket, quite a large amount and £50 in notes. At first she thought he had stolen it off Roy but Roy knew nothing about it. She had asked Roy if he knew anything about Billy's activities but apart from paying him to go out once a week Roy could not recall anything he had said about his lifestyle. How did she know so little about her own son?

The police put a broadcast out on the early evening news for anyone who had been with Billy in the last thirty six hours. Several school children came forward but none of his mates replied from the estate. The teachers and Tanya and her two friends called the police, scared. They were interviewed by a woman officer with Tanya's Dad in tow which did not help. "Tanya," said WPC Mari Coomber, "when did you first meet Billy?" "At school" she muttered nervously. "We went for a milkshake on Monday and Tuesday and sat in a café for an hour." Tanya was recoiling with nerves in front of her father. "What sort of relationship did you have?" More nerves. "It wasn't a relationship. We just talked about music tracks. We were going to swap CDs that's all." "Is there anything Billy said or did that may indicate where he got infected?"

Tanya hesitated. "Well he did talk a lot about zombies and things and how to turn people into them." "Can you explain that a bit more in detail?" tried Mari. "He said there was a gang he belonged to. The leader was that guy, Jake or something, who died of plague before. Billy said he was going to be the next leader." "He said Jake had given him the Leaders ring." Mari was alert. "A ring? What was it like? Did he show you?" Mari was aware that if there was any link between Jake and Billy it could be the key to the mystery. Tanya tried to remember. "It was big, too big for him, blue in the middle and white bits round the outside. It was silver, the actual ring, really old looking. He said Jake said he was giving it to him because he knew he was going to die." "He knew he was going to die?" "That's what Billy said. Jake said 'take it in case anything happens to me' but that is just what Billy said. I didn't really believe him."

Mari was aware her every word was being recorded and listened to by DCI Mustoe so needed to make sure she asked everything clearly. "So what did Billy think he was leader of?" "Some sort of secret group, just blokes, no girls. They met up in something they called the bunker." Mari said "yes we know about the bunker, it's all locked up now. Did you ever go to the bunker with him?" "Of course not; I only spoke to him on Monday for the first time. I told you we just met in a cafe. Ask my friends." Mari felt sorry for her. She must be scared that she had spoken to him quite closely. "I'm sorry Tanya but we just need to know every detail if we can. You're doing really well." Tanya's father gasped with frustration. "I suppose you realise she could be infected? Can't you see how scared she is?" Mari kept her cool. "I know how worrying this is but Tanya has been tested and we have to wait for results but the condition can only be infectious if it is transmitted through blood."

"I haven't had any blood contact with anyone," squealed Tanya. "Good, so you're not at risk. Did he have the ring on his finger?" "He had it in his pocket and brought it out to show me, then he put it on his finger. He didn't have it on today though." "Did he say why not?" "No he just did not have it on." "Right Tanya if you could just wait here a short while with your Dad. Do you want a drink?" She asked the staff to get Tanya and her father tea although they had not asked for it. She went back to Mustoe and Benson. "Is that enough?" Looks like the ring has some sort of infection in it. Billy must have stolen it off Jake. If that was the first time Billy wore it it's had effect in 24 hours. That ties in with the prognosis by Dr Champion."

Benson turned to Mustoe when Mari returned. "We need to find that ring. Billy's unconscious, we'll have to ask Evie." Mark went over to Gloucester Royal and gowned up to see Evie. "Hi Evie, how is it going?" She looked shell shocked. "I'm fine but I don't think Billy is going to pull through. Look at him he's grey and fevered up. She started to sob. "Is there someone we should inform? Someone to be with you?" "No there was only me an' Billy. His Dad's in prison. He's all I've got." She started sobbing uncontrollably. "It's that bastard Jake is to blame. I always said he was trouble." "I'm sorry Evie but there are some questions we need to ask."

"Did Billy have any rings? Did you see him wearing a ring ever?" Evie shook her head. "Only his girlfriend says he had it on Monday as it may have caused the injury to his finger. It was a big blue stone with white stones round the outside. A man's ring." "Billy didn't have any rings. He was only fifteen. We haven't got money for rings." Evie was convinced Billy had been out burgling houses. £50? Cannabis resin? big rings? He had been out every night. Now she knew what he and that Jake were up to. "Mrs Smith, we need to search Billy's room for that ring. He may have other things that explain how he got this disease. Do we need to get a warrant?

Evie shook her head. She had no concern about the house being searched when Billy was dying before her eyes. "No go on. I may not have a son tomorrow." If it saves someone else's life…."

The police took Evie's keys and were there in twenty minutes. They methodically searched the room; white clad soccos in steri-suits and hoods. Every drawer, every pile of clothes; the boards were taken up, the wallpaper searched for secret panels. Benson felt aggravated.

"It's not a Tudor Manor House, it's a council flat. There's no room for secret panels in here. The walls are paper thin." After an hour they all sat back on their heels, perplexed. The PC on duty at the door looked in at their puzzled faces. "Scuse me Sir but when I did a placement at Gloucester Gaol they said prisoners always stuffed things in the bed frame." Two soccos leapt up and started dismantling the hollow metal tubular frame. There it was. The ring was wrapped in tissue along with about £200 and two bags of resin. "Promotion for PC Davies!" Shouted Benson.

The items were bagged, the room sealed and they headed off to the pathology lab. They did not need to be told it was the key to the mystery. Penny Worstham, Mari Coomber and Mustoe sat on their desks having received the phone call from the Smiths flat confirming Billy's possession of the ring. Mustoe summarized what they knew for certain. "We know he got the ring from Jake. Jake dies of plague. Now Billy's infected on the ring finger. Both of them meet up in the bunker or Jake's flat. The ring is old, possibly hundreds of years old. Either Jake robbed it or he dug it up somewhere. The bunker is underground; I reckon he dug it up there." Penny spoke. "But we've been in there. All there is is a pile of porn mags and plastic crates. He told Annie he had got something that would keep on paying." Mustoe was beginning to see the way. "We'll have to look at that bunker again." Get on to the soccos and tell them to stay there."

The soccos who had been at Billy's flat were sent back again and despatched up to the aerodrome. The pensioners in Meadows Drive saw the blue lights go past in the dark, this time by-passing the estate and winding their way over the rough track through the field and up to the bunker, erecting a yellow tent over it. The steel door remained in place and they unlocked the padlocked hinges, shone in their lamps and let themselves down the metal ladder. Sergeant Benson and DI Mustoe sat in the doorway with the overview.

"What have we missed? Look at that earth floor, pick up that bit of lino. Any sign the floors have been dug up?" They carefully pulled up layers of old lino covering the dirt floor. It revealed a concrete base barely covered in soil and hardly scratched in fifty years. "What are the walls made of?" There were wooden boards attached to a wood framework round the walls and when removed it revealed the original concrete sleepers. DI Mustoe shone his torch to the end wall. "What about that end panel?" The lamps swiveled to the rear of the bunker. All the debris had been removed now, the old car seats, the magazines, the cushions, all was laid bare. The socco put his white gloved hands on the top of the old wooden door. "Looks like it's an old door been put here. Help us pull the bottom up." They wedged a jemmy under the door and levered and the whole panel fell away from the wall. What they saw beyond made them jump back. As the panel came back in their hands they dropped it on the floor revealing a cavity about two feet back of damp soil seeping liquid on to the floor beyond. In the moist soil they could see white fragments, which one of the soccos bent to examine.

"Christ! Its finger bones!" They leapt back and shone the torches on to the hole. More rotted bones were evident, crumbling away in the soil, spilling out into the bunker, disintegrating as they watched. Slowly one by one, they backed out of the bunker, crawled up the ladder and stood outside, shocked and repulsed.

Behind them Benson called in the forensic service. "This could be a big one. It's definitely a graveyard and we'll need big guns up here with protection."

CHAPTER SIXTEEN

AFTERMATH

BILLY'S DEATH AFFECTED everyone on the estate. Not only was he well known, as were the other youths but he had a cheeky something about him that even the retired residents of Meadows Drive could forgive him his crimes. He had some indescribable life force that had encouraged others to take a hold on life even if it was into illegality and his demise put out another little flame of hope for the rest. Evie was dumbstruck. The police had arranged a support worker to sit with her, also hoping to glean some indication of his friends and whereabouts before he took ill. Billy's two sisters were interviewed by a social worker about what they knew of Billy's lifestyle and friends but they were overwhelmed with grief and could not say much. The social worker advised they be given time to recover.

Whilst Evie had loved her son without a stop she had also taken their relationship for granted. She had tried her best but she knew the life she had given Billy was not a good one even if she had taught him manners and morals, the pull of his acquaintance was much stronger. She had expected a life of visiting him in prison, the baby due before he was 16, caring for his partner's children and endless calls from the police before Billy moved into some young woman's flat and stayed.

The worst she feared was heroin. While she knew Billy knocked about with some rough ones it was only Jake's influence she feared and when he died she had difficulty repressing the relief she felt. Jake must be someone's son, someone's baby, yet she could not find compassion enough to forgive him introducing the lads to drugs and crime as she believed he had done. She had to face it, Jake was Billy in 10 years time. She was surprised to hear that Jake was not a heroin addict. He looked like one. When Billy was so stunned at his death she wondered if he had some sexual connection with Jake. She shuddered to think that whatever killed him may have been passed on to Billy this way.

Roy came round to look after her but she was inconsolable. She sat still staring into space, dimmed by the sedating drugs given to her by the doctor. Intermittently a picture of Billy with Jake would cross her mind and she would convulse again into sobs. The thought that other people would always now associate the two people together made her want to rail against the injustice, run out in the street and tell everyone what a great son he was, what a sweet child he had been but no one was interested. Even Roy found it hard to manage her grief and went back and forth to his home every so often with a dive into the pub between. It was far too early to discuss funerals and arrangements. After all what arrangements had to be made for a child? The vicar came twice to offer consolation but Evie, whilst wanting to shriek out her grief was dumb still. The words were not big enough to express how she felt.

On the day after Billy's death DI Mustoe and DS Benson stood in the mortuary gowned and masked behind a screen. The pathologist who worked alone was in rubber from head to foot and looked through a glass fronted mask. They had now identified the type of infection as bubonic plague, a disease that had not existed in Britain for two centuries, but lurked elsewhere in the world. There seemed to be no explanation of how a 14 year old boy in a remote housing estate in Gloucester with no contacts in China or South America could catch the disease, even if it was as a result of contact with Jake, the path of transmission would have to be body fluids. Even the care worn Mustoe had difficulty believing that Billy was in a sexual relationship with Jake. Mustoe had heard tales of Marj McCormack, he knew Billy had had girls on his mind. His room was full of posters of the Debbie Harry and Bananarama. He was a fair faced boy with a cheeky grin, no problem with attracting the girls there.

The pathologist raised his head and pointed at Billy's finger. Mustoe and Benson craned forward to look. There was a suppurating sore on Billy's ring finger which had swollen into a purple blister. Through a fuzzy microphone he said "This is the point of entry, no doubt. Was there a ring found on the body?" He turned to the mortuary assistant also gowned but well away from the body. "No Sir, it was hidden in his room." Mustoe was agitated, "Anyone could have tried on that ring. Someone else could have worn it between Billy and Jake and be out there with the plague."

He needed intelligence. Who was friends with Jake? Had they used the ring? Or any other artefact that could be contaminated? He needed an expert view on the type of ring it was. He ordered Benson "go back to the office, get Penny Worstham and go back to Dursley and interview every boy who was friends with Billy, and that Frankie girl Penny was so interested in". He paused. He needed to get this right and quickly. If he did not act now and get the right answers and someone else died he would be on the front of every Sunday paper in the country as the officer in charge who got it wrong. He felt his forehead break out in a sweat. "Oh and Benson, get an expert on old rings, someone recommended by Scotland Yard, we can't afford to make a mistake on this one".

Billy's funeral was well attended considering he had not been favoured either by his school or his neighbours. His school friends hung about the crematorium in Gloucester, even the boys visibly moved by the horror of his death. Nick and Eddy had blagged a lift from Roy in his Ford Cortina and although they arrived in style they were overcome by the knowledge it could have been one of them.

"He was a good lad Billy, never harmed no one in his life. Only nicked off people who could afford it." Said Nick. "He never told us about nicking Jake's ring. It could have been one of us put it on. What if he had showed us an' we all put it on. We'd all be done for," added Eddy. "Billy was secretive. We didn't know till after he'd done Jake's flat. He had all the stash as well as the ring an' never told us."

Billy's mother, Evie, was consumed with grief. All her life she had tried to protect him from his violent father, unreliable men and passing boyfriends she could have had;

dangerous neighbours and gang members and now he had died of the plague. He would be notorious. Billy's father had got permission to attend the funeral on compassionate grounds and stood there with his hands cuffed to a prison guard. They had had to cremateBilly's body from the morgue in a body bag and she could not even prepare him with his favourite trainers and kit as she wanted. No one could see him before he died. To Evie it was the worst shock of all; she could not touch his hand or kiss him goodbye at the last.

Marj McCormack came to the service. Her flowery pink dress reminiscent of the dressing gown she always wore indoors. A quarter of a bottle of gin in her handbag lubricated the tears and real sadness for the loss of her little Billy. Many were the boys she had "educated" over the years but Billy had been special to her, a fun loving boy who never judged or scolded her like some of the others had done; to be sure he had a generous heart.

The press were there in droves, the News of the World and The People in particular. There was hardly a youth from Stonefield or Little Meadows who was not queueing up for a handout in exchange for a tit bit about Billy's past. And there were plenty of stories. The following Sunday Evie's neighbours intervened to warn her not to buy the papers as Billy was now famous for his criminal exploits rather than his unique demise. Evie took the papers home and cried and cried at the stories, many could not have been true, surely, of Billy in his fourteen years. They had interviewed classmates she had never heard of as well as local thugs she did not even know he knew. She wondered if she had ever known her son at all.

Marj went home and drowned her sorrows in a gallon of scrumpy, shared with Nick and Eddy but there were no games in the bedroom that day.

PC Wortham and DC Benson sat in the back of the crematorium throughout the service. They had seen a community exposed, contaminated, quarantined and bereaved and through it all found some endearing qualities in those they had previously dismissed as worthless. There had been some positives. Frankie was now receiving counselling and addiction treatment, the flats were now officially condemned and due to be totally rebuilt, after all who would want to move into a plague infested building?

The bunker was being excavated by a forensic archeologist, all in sealed suits and breathing masks. They removed the earth above the bunker finding only the rotten wooden walls and the corrugated tin roof. They dug down four feet where the bones had been exposed in the bunker to find the remains of Squire Martyn; some very fragile bones, a gold chain and some silver buttons. The pearls had disintegrated, the cuffs and ruffs and brocade long ago melted away bar a few gold threads in the dirt that had been Squire Martyn's waistcoat. One silver buckle from his shoe was found, the other not in evidence.

To their surprise they had not found any more bodies, supposing the bunker had been dug next to a plague pit. They expected to find many bodies, possibly all tipped in together and the single body was so unexpected that they decided to study the records of Worsley going back to the seventeenth century.

In 1489 a merchant from Plymouth had built a hall house on the site where now stood the single runway of the aerodrome. Rough hewn stone from the local quarry with outbuildings and its demesne would have been several acres of fields and plough land a mile or so from Worsley village. In the 1600s the property had been handed on to an heir who further developed his business interests in trade and sold the land on to another tradesman dealing in wool. The Worsley Hall that Suzannah would have known was built on to the old house using local stone and the front elevation and utilities providing a reception hall and parlour with fireplaces. When Suzannah arrived the house was virtually new and in splendid condition. Squire Martyn had purchased it with his trade money in 1642, the year Oliver Cromwell had achieved a Republic but having no allegiance to monarchy Martyn was favoured and got trade through the political changes that he supported. His devoutly Presbyterian wife also enhanced his status with the New Parliament. By the 1660s the restored King had forgiven his errant subjects and held no grudge against merchants who filled the coffers with their taxes. He had encouraged trade and supported a growing wealth to all who did not wish to thwart his reign and again Squire Martyn's fortunes looked good.

Twenty four years after he bought the Hall, Martyn, bloated and sated with wealth and the oppression of his fellow humans, had disappeared on his way back from a journey to Bristow, assumed to have been beset by robbers. According to the Court Rolls a Magistrate had dealt with Squire Martyn's disappearance. Squire Martyn's son Daniel was twelve when his father disappeared in 1688, his memory being eclipsed by news of the seizing of Bristow ships illegally trading in slaves weeks later. Mr Fenwick lost his ship "the

Betty" for illegal slave trading but managed to rescue his business none the less.

Fortunately Rebecca's brother-in-law, Charles, managed to arrange for Daniel Martyn to follow Richard into an Oxford College and to study law and, with his uncles and cousins as good examples, he sloughed off the taint of the Martyns and made a good life in business law. By the age of twenty four he began to take an interest in politics and the views of liberal men and joined the campaign to abolish slavery. Although he was lambasted for his fortune having been made from slavery his oratorical skills were such that he could support the cause and maintain his wealth while donating much benefit to schools and almshouses for the poor. When Rebecca died in 1694 and his sisters were well married to local gentlemen he had the house demolished and the stone used to build a new school in Worsley. There were scholarships for children up to the age of twelve so that farm labourers could aspire to greater things by way of an education. Daniel moved to Bath when Bath was becoming a fine Georgian town fit for an educated and socially aware gentleman and flourished.

The lands of Worsley Hall were sold off piecemeal to local landowners and the site of the house remained unusable for farmland with the foundations of the house left behind. The two wells were filled in and the area retained a melancholy that was not explicable to locals but it was generally accepted that no one wanted to live there at all.

In later years rumour had it that the well water had been contaminated and when the stream dried up there was no source of clean water. Others recalled hearing their ancestors saying there had been a curse on the family and that the widow of Squire Martyn had never shaken off the blight of having a husband who had disappeared mysteriously. The favourite story was that he had taken a mistress in Bristow and sailed to the West Indies and lived there as man and wife, denying his previous marriage at all.

That any man should abandon his son and heir was unthinkable but the story gained much credibility from Squire Martyn's gaming friends who knew all too well of his wife's coldness towards him and his bragging about a young beauty who had come into his life in recent years.

In 1941 the Americans had rolled into Britain to fight the war in Europe and aerodromes were built all over Gloucestershire to launch attacks on the Nazis. If they dug through the tilth of arable fields and discovered the solid foundations of Worsley Hall no one was much interested at that time and a sea of concrete was poured over the land. The bunker was dug out rapidly as once the aircraft were in place it attracted constant onslaught from enemy bombers. Another three feet to one side and Squire Martyn's bones would never have been discovered then and Jake and Billy need never have died.

CHAPTER SEVENTEEN

RESOLUTION

SUZANNAH HAD GROWN from a naive teenager to a hardened woman capable of hiding secret knowledge. She knew now what lusts men possessed and how to satisfy them. She knew what callous and cruel hearts some men sheltered in their breasts and how their colleagues and patrons corrupted young men to believe such oppression was acceptable. Disinclined to attach herself to any man after the horrors of Squire Martyn's death she attached herself to Rebecca, both concealing the knowledge of his burial and she felt obliged to support her in her widowhood, and appeared to all around her to remain a maid. Despite the Restoration, Rebecca's household remained doggedly puritan and prayers and parsimony were the order of the day.

In 1693 Rebecca took a turn for the worst and although Suzannah sat with her and bathed her fevered body, a proper nurse, ordered by the physician, came to take responsibility. Ann Friend was now elderly and paid off and given an alms house in the town and Suzannah took on the role of housekeeper. They had no visitors and much of the farm work was overseen by the bailiff. Suzannah had little to do but check the laundry, oversee the washing, cleaning, brewing, storing of crops. Now Daniel had finished his studies and over eighteen he was increasingly taking charge of the family wealth and investing in new ventures abroad that did not involve slavery. He was such a staunch opponent that much of his profit was given to missions in London which housed disabled seamen, often blacks who had seen service on ships.

Suzannah felt this life of deprivation was the only way she could atone for her sins to God and to Rebecca and neither of them spoke of it again. Rebecca's reluctance to eat or enjoy life meant she was often sickly and weak and Suzannah sat often and long at her bedside to the end, comforting her and reading the bible. At her last breath Rebecca squeezed Suzannah's hand and whispered "Thankyou for what you did for me," and both knew it was not the last few years she was referring to.

Once released from her charge when Maria married and her sister Catherine two years later, Suzannah stayed with Rebecca as her maid and companion. She was twenty three and while she was trim and gold haired there was a weariness about her that meant the local men overlooked her for younger girls and as no man called at Worsley Hall she met no one new. She was at liberty to go home frequently and although she rarely saw Constance, she and her mother, now grey haired and plump, sat by the fire, sewing and embroidering linen as the light lasted.

"My Suzannah, I'd have thought you the first to marry of all my girls but you have shown no interest in all these years. Surely you wish to have children of your own?

"Mother I have seen much of married life and Rebecca has been an example to me of piety and constancy. I no longer see the world through the eyes of avarice and greed and I have come to understand the value of friendship and what a marriage should be". She meditated on the once held desire to marry a businessman from Bristow and how the misery of others would then have played on her conscience.

"You and father are an example I should follow should I meet the right partner."

As Rebecca declined and Suzannah visited home weekly she spent more time with her brothers and uncle's families and the journeyman, Hugh, who had barely a farthing when they first met was now taken into the business. Quiet and devout they also met when he attended church on his infrequent returns to Worsley and by the time she was twenty five were old acquaintance. So much so that they would sit outside the cottage on summer evenings alone and happy to enjoy God's gifts of harvest and sunsets and warmth.

Rebecca's death changed everything. Not only was there not a role for Suzannah at the house but Daniel was planning to demolish the premises and cut loose from the reputation of his family in local memory and use the wealth to do good. Suzannah was at a loss to know what to do. She would have joined a priory but despite her devotion to duty she felt no desire to marry the church. If she went home, her status would have been compromised as there was no role for her there either. Her married sisters would find some occupation for her but she would always be an appendage in their homes, a burden on their husbands. But one day her father came to her with a proposal.

"Young Hugh has been a friend and our journeyman these five years and has proved himself a loyal and diligent servant. He has now been given his just reward in being taken into our business and will benefit from the profits of our wool and cloth. He has asked my permission for your hand in marriage and I wonder what you think to that?"

Suzannah smiled at her father's straightforwardness. She was not surprised but unable to think about it initially. Rebecca's death, her discomfort at the part she played in hiding Squire Martyn's demise made such a decision unbearable. However after a week's contemplation she arranged to meet with Hugh for a formal discussion. He pledged his commitment to marry and spoke of the admiration he had for her piety and devotion to God and her mistress. Suzannah hinted at her doubts of being suitable after so long being a servant and spinster but in one word he put her mind at rest.

"My dearest Suzannah I was but a callow youth when first I saw you as a girl and I loved you then. But I knew you to be desirous of seeing the world and to experience life outside of a small town and the confines of a close knit family. You were exposed, I believe, to the evils of a world corrupted by greed and heartlessness by other men but you came through. Whatever you have suffered at the hands of this worldly exposure I can accept because I know you have seen this life and rejected it wholeheartedly. All of us deserve God's good grace, the opportunity to learn from our experiences and grow into good hearted and grateful pilgrims and having absorbed God's wisdom and goodness to bless others with our experience. Will you start your new life with me?"

There was nothing more to be said. Suzannah knew that all her past sins would be forgiven by such a godly man and suspected he knew a good deal of what she had endured. They married in April, under a startling blue sky and rented a small house in the main street. Daniel bought their marriage bed and donated many things from Worsley Hall, being wealthy enough to refurbish his new house in Bath with the latest fashions.

They were taken into the company of her uncle and introduced to the Guild where they were feted. Suzannah gave birth to two beautiful children at the late age of twenty seven. She gave her navy velvet dress, packed away these five years, to the parish, sold her jewellery and when Daniel had the Hall dismantled and used the money to build the Church School she donated the rest of her silver to good causes and the education of the poor children of the Parish.

THE END